WHAT IT MEANS TO LOVE YOU

A Novel by Stephen Elliott

MacAdam/Cage Publishing
155 Sansome Street, Suite 550
San Francisco, CA 94104
www.macadamcage.com

Library of Congress Cataloging-in-Publication Data

Elliott, Stephen, 1971–
    What it means to love you / by Stephen Elliott.
        p. cm.
    ISBN 1-931561-18-4 (hardback : alk. paper)
    1. Triangles (Interpersonal relations)–Fiction. 2. Chicago
    (Ill.)–Fiction. 3. Slums–Fiction. I. Title.
    PS3605.L46 W48 2002
    813'.6–dc21

                                                2002005900

Book design and cover photography by Dorothy Carico Smith.

WHAT IT MEANS
TO LOVE YOU

A Novel by Stephen Elliott

MacAdam/Cage

Tom Vitaich 1966–2001

For my publisher, David Poindexter

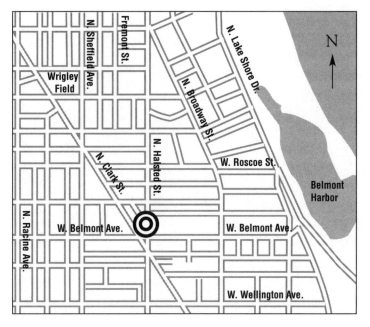

NEWTOWN, CHICAGO

THERE WAS a storm that lowered itself over a city and it drenched the buildings and made the streets shine beneath the lamps. The streets became hypnotic. The colors popped from the stop signs and the fire hydrants. The rain pushed the trash and the people inside for cover. They knew the rain was never going to stop. The rain cleaned the air so all I could smell was you. The rain smacked across the roofs and all I could hear was you. The rain came in tight clouds, hovering in and caressing the sky. It was only going to rain forever. What it means to love you. It is the end of the seasons, the end of the earth. It is impossible. It flutters through my fingers, harder to hold than air. It falls across the rocks, rattles the leaves, melts the ice and the snow. It is the tiniest tip of the skyscrapers in the cities and the running gutters and the parks. That is what it means to love you. It is the end of loneliness. The loneliness that haunts me. That returns when you are in the bathroom, when you go to the store, when you look away. You carry my stomach with you and leave me with a hole when you are gone. The loneliness is in my walls, in my skin. I can't wash it out. You pour over me. You drown me. I wait on you for my breath. Nobody could ever die for you the way that I die for you. The only thing worse than loving you is not loving you, and that is what it means.

HALSTED STREET brims with atmosphere rising from the shelters and the lights of Boys Town. The fags and the hags and the queens and the yuppies and the kids fresh out of college looking for something true. And the new millionaires with pushed-back wavy brown hair, cashing in stock for twisted nights around storefront strip clubs. And hookers hooking for tips. And grease-filled fag magnets, dirty pink triangles turning meat for crack and salvation, and the sports bars with a view of Wrigley Field and all-night coffee shops, the *Clack Clack Clack* of see-through heels, all brim on Halsted Street in Chicago, a coffeepot full of atmosphere.

There are many different reasons for migrating to Halsted Street. Every night the children run away from home to sit in front of Dunkin' Donuts. They come from Morton Grove, Skokie, Oak Park, and Evanston. They ask people for quarters. They sit with radios along the curb playing the latest tunes. They dance to the music when the sidewalks are clear, stomping their feet and raising curled fists to their foreheads. Most of the kids are just slumming, booking on some boring suburban existence. They choose the cement and neon over the bright green lawns and some boring suburban school that justifies their parents' boring lives when their parents tell their friends, "We moved here for the better schools." The kids run from the boring suburban schools and arrive at Belmont and Halsted, and the promised pink and white lights of the Dunkin' Donuts shop. They dye their hair blue, wear cheap spiked bracelets purchased at the Alley. Some of the kids sew swastikas on their jackets and others sew anti-Nazi patterns. This is why they fight. The kids sew up black pants with other black pants, a competition of patches. The kids just want to know who can get closer to what it means to be real.

Some of the kids are already there. Some of the kids run away every morning and don't go back. They are real runaways from abusive parents up on the North Side, rebels from heroin houses and crack parents on the West Side. Some of them contemplate accepting rides in passing cars. For them Halsted is not an adventure but a place they can go. They sleep at the Neon Street Children's Shelter. They eat what they are given. Any home is better than the home they left behind.

There are many different reasons for migrating to Halsted Street. Freshly graduated students with their first jobs Downtown punching numbers for Arthur Andersen, interning for Blau Direct, first-year lawyers at Sidley and Austin, all move into Lakeview, to experience the city. They work in cubicles during the day behind five-foot walls of fabric, drowning in benefits and worthless stock options. They are account executives, project managers, marketing associates. They work in the John Hancock Building, the Sears Tower, the Standard Oil Building, and 100 Upper Wacker Drive. The day steals their privacy and the night gives it back. They find themselves combing Halsted Street, hands in the pockets of their jeans, college sweatshirts blowing in the stiff wind. Late at night with twenties stuck to their fingers and sweat along their foreheads they find themselves roaming the top floors of yellow-lit buildings with broken doors where they simply should not be.

Queers from all over the Midwest move to Boys Town on Halsted Street so they can dance in Roscoe's and be accepted. They end up in the ManHole on lights-out night walking around the pitch-black club in their underwear, swimming in a K-hole, their balls groped, grabbed, and squeezed. They meet at Eros and walk in naked wearing white towels on Sunday afternoon and suck each other off in private rooms with milk-colored plastic saucers full of condoms on the nightstand. Boys Town is paradise and the flags of the revolution fly over the light poles. The queers staff the AIDS hotline and crisis office. They come home from Downtown smelling nice and well-manicured in long wool coats ready to see a play at the Turn Around Theater on Halsted and Grove.

The homeless lurk along the edge of the Triangle on Halsted Street. They beg for noodles in front of Penny's. They follow pedestrians, hands stretched forward, scabs on their arms and their faces. They get needles, soup, and medical attention in Uptown. They sleep in cardboard boxes next to the Walgreens.

The trannies migrate to Halsted and Broadway in tight glittering shorts and high heels showing off their long legs and strong calves. The trannies' best light is the light of the Treasure Island sign. The Treasure Island light is always on, holding over a large gourmet grocery store that sells food in fancy brown paper bags. Treasure Island is open from eight in the morning until ten at night when the fun begins. After ten the trannies fill the parking lot, faces thick with make-up, hair wrapped in tight buns over their heads. The trannies walk tall, breasts poking through sweaters, defying the wind. The trannies beat the college boys in the alleys with the college boys' belts while the college boys lick the heels of their shoes. The trannies escort college boys to the ATM next to the vitamin shop, then paint lipstick on the boys' mouths, then they make them say terrible things, and the college boys run home desperately wiping their lips with their T-shirts until their lips are raw and bleeding. The trannies blow Jons for twenty-five bucks or for ten. The trannies blow Jons in the bathroom at the Vortex. The trannies blow anybody for any price. They spend the days fitting into their clothes and the nights selling it all as quickly as they come without answering any uncomfortable questions. They do it along Halsted Street with glitter and wigs and silicone. They do it until the morning when they go to work Downtown crunching numbers for large accounting firms or they hole up in some cheap hotel next to the video game parlor to get high. And if they have an addiction they sleep off what is left at the Wellington Shelter underneath the red brick church. The streets embrace the trannies in their arms, and save them from certain slaughter.

Anthony walks tight-shouldered down Halsted Street, his balled fists stuffed deep into the pockets of his jeans, the sharp lines on his face pointing forward. The fall has tripped across Chicago, erasing the summer and the headlines full of old people dying as the heatwave stretched its fingers into the air-conditioning units in a strip of third-rate peeling brown nursing homes. The fall cold bites at Anthony's clear white cheeks.

Anthony's long curly blond hair blows behind him in bright platinum streaks bleached from hot summers on the rocks at Lake Michigan. Long earrings dangle from either ear. He walks purposely, his head down. His compact body gives off an illusion of being short for 5'9".

He passes the pool hall near Addison. Inside a handful of thirtysomethings play pool and pass around pitchers of beer.

Everything is looking up for Lakewood. Anthony pushes his hair away from his face, and stops at the window to watch a girl lean over the pool table. She pushes her ass out and draws her stick back. She swings her stick and the cue ball rolls along the green into the nine ball and one ball almost drops. One of the men says something and she laughs and the others laugh as well. She goes to a thin round table with another girl and two boys. They all wear sweaters and drink beer from eight-ounce glasses. Anthony stares at them and makes up stories for their lives. He leans toward the window as one of the men leans closely to a girl and whispers something in her ear. She laughs and pushes him away while keeping an arm around his waist. The four make numerous toasts, speaking loudly, showing off clean, white teeth and taking small sips on their glasses of beer. Anthony pushes his fingers along the windowpane, feels the heat coming through from the warm bar.

Anthony straightens himself up. He notices the bar clock, lit with an orange neon glow. He leaves the people in the bar and marches off to his destination down Halsted Street. Deep down on Halsted Street.

It is not easy to notice the Stolen Pony. Nobody walks into the Stolen Pony unintentionally. There is no sign over the bar, just a neon horseshoe on the thin black window. It stands squeezed and unassuming between a diner and a vintage furniture store. Nobody knows about the Stolen Pony who doesn't want to. The Stolen Pony does not take out ads or sponsor events, does not maintain a float in the Pride Parade. The Stolen Pony is a tiny bar on a busy strip of Halsted Street that fully occupies an entire world.

The door closes behind Anthony and takes the last of

the day's sunlight with it. The bar is shaped like an S with three round tables off to the side and a small square stage in the middle. The S-shaped bar is a couple of feet wide and sticky and black. There is only one beer tap, the rest of the beer is in bottles. Cheap bottles of liquor stand on a shelf in disarray. Behind the bar hangs a large mirror tilting forward, stained with brown and white spots, like someone had intentionally sprayed the mirror with Champagne. Anthony smells the familiar stench of being in the wrong place at the wrong time.

Sitting at the bar are men: fat, skinny, one with a fading brown mustache, another with pockmarked cheeks, still another with a long, sharp, pointy nose. They wear their clothes badly, all of them. Their pants don't fit. The men are not shaped right; their shoulders slouch; they are curved wrong. One man wears a lavender corduroy shirt. Another wears a turquoise polo one size too small and rests his hand on an open newspaper that another is also fingering the edges of. Still another wears bright orange pants.

Henry, the bartender, smacks his towel against the bar with a loud, wet snap and the man with the beak-like nose lets out a short, breathy laugh. A large stereo, typical of the type that sells for forty dollars at garage sales, hangs precariously on a thin rope above the mirror. *You never need to walk away until you've gone too far…*

Henry is a large man with an awful, fat face like a baby grown to six feet tall. All of his features are just like a newborn's, squinty eyes, rolls of fat hugging his eyebrows, short, pudgy fingers. On his head he wears a golden tiara.

"You must be Anthony," he says. The men watch carefully, clutching their drinks. "My name is Henry. I own the Stolen Pony. This is my kingdom and stretches as far as the eyes can see to the north, south, east, and west." Henry covers the bar with one sweeping fat arm. "Welcome to my kingdom, Anthony. On behalf of the Stolen Pony and its subjects, I adore you." Henry yanks a man's glass off the bar and sticks it under the only spout, filling it with yellow foam.

The lights go down. Anthony climbs the two steps to the stage barefoot. Small lights overhead cover the stage with thin yellow wattage. The stage itself is made up of translucent colored square lights that shoot slowly up Anthony's legs in pale shades of pink and blue. Their mutterings quiet down as the music gets louder.

Anthony waves as best he can to the music. It's a small stage with not much room to move. The lights blink on and off beneath him. The light blues tighten his chin. He lifts his shirt over his head, flexes his biceps. Goosebumps pop on his naked, freshly shaven chest. Somebody walks in the door and a cold breeze cuts across the room. Anthony cannot see from the stage. The men are dark silhouettes. The bar is a million miles away. Anthony's long hair covers his cold, naked shoulders.

The stage sticks beneath Anthony's feet. He lays on his back, stares to the ceiling lights. The colored squares engulf his body. The colored squares swallow Anthony. He rolls his pants down his legs.

"Take it all off," one of the men yells. "Take it all off, Anthony." They already know his name.

"Don't listen to him, Anthony," Henry corrects. "You know the rules."

Anthony slips the pants over his feet and kicks them to the floor. He dances around, only a black thong left. He knows the rules. He's been around long enough. He bucks his

hips against the cold square lights and against the silhou-
etted stares of the bar. He feels the cold plastic of the colored
lights against his naked back, pressing the back of his thighs.
He is still grinding and pushing his hips against the stage
when the music fades and the lights come on.

The men are whistling and clapping as Anthony gathers
his clothes. Twelve dollars lay scattered in small, crumpled
bills across the stage. Anthony grabs the money and pulls on
his jeans, quickly stuffing the money into his pockets. He
walks past the bar and into the back room.

In the back there are long, thin pieces of glass. The extra
liquor is locked in cages. Wooden shelves are bolted to the
walls and held by chains and nylon cords alternately from
the ceiling. At a large wooden table Henry lays down a contract for Anthony to sign; a mouse or a rat scampers over
Anthony's foot. Dusty kegs line the walls and one thick
plastic tube runs out to the bar. A pair of shoes sits on one of
the plywood shelves next to a balled-up pair of underwear.
The back room smells of old beer and sweet perfume and
spilled, sticky drinks heavy with syrup. The back room is
flooded with harsh yellow light. Coming off the stage, it
seems to Anthony like the ugliest place in the world.

"You can't dance anywhere else," Henry says. "You know
that, don't you? We like to think of ourselves as an exclusive
club."

Anthony smells the air. He takes in Henry's fat features,
Henry's eyebrows drooping over his eyes, cocks his head.
Henry's demands are absurd. Anthony knows the Stolen
Pony. Anthony is thirty-four years old. He has been in places
like this before. He knows this is the bottom of the barrel.
This is not an exclusive club. This is a place old men come

to when they have nowhere else to go. They come here because they are lonely, without enough money to take a boy back to their rooms. They come here to pick up boys and they make them promises they can't keep. Dancers for their part dance here because they are not quite beautiful enough. They are not tall enough to be models. They are not thick enough for Chippendales. And they can't do anything else. They have just missed and they know it. And sometimes just missing is worse than never having a chance at all. They come here for fifty dollars a shift plus tips. They come to the Stolen Pony to blow customers for one hundred dollars between sets down at the Ram. They come here for easy money to support habits or they come here because they are too lazy to move boxes, to work in a warehouse, too vain to wear a red apron at some fast food restaurant. Anthony knows why people dance at the Stolen Pony. You're like that chicken they sell in Domicks for half-price, he thinks. Covered in barbecue sauce. You do what you can.

"You can't dance anywhere else," Henry continues. "And between sets we expect you to hang out at the bar. We don't want you sitting back here moping. And if you're not talking to a customer you can pick up glasses and help keep the place clean. But you shouldn't sit down. Leave the seats for our patrons. And pay them attention. People like attention."

Anthony stares up at Henry's fat face and laughs. Then he scribbles his name across the bottom of the page.

Henry grabs Anthony's face in his enormous hands. "Welcome to my family," he says. Henry lowers his face to Anthony's and presses his teeth against Anthony's earlobe. "I will raise you like a son."

2

THE TAXIS criss-cross Chicago's highways and loop through Downtown and the Near West Side. They funnel through Downtown and connect with Lake Shore Drive and Lake Michigan via Lower Wacker Drive and Congress Parkway. Lake Shore Drive runs past the shining black McCormick Center, the young Mayor Daley's present to the union bosses, and then loops quickly past the Field Museum of Natural History and Soldier Field, where the Chicago Bears play. Lake Shore Drive touches the edge of the Museum of Science and Industry and the University of Chicago. The 294 separates the Robert Taylor Homes from Bridgeport, the senior Mayor Daley's present to his white constituency, separating the black South Side from the white South Side, an unnatural border built to stop the two groups from killing one another. The 290 nearly slams right into Midway Airport. The Edens Expressway whips neatly around O'Hare International, the busiest airport in the world.

Surrounding O'Hare gleaming hotels sparkle in the sparse suburban skyline. Beyond the hotels small bungalows stand in brown rows on tree-lined streets like ears of corn. They send endless complaints toward city hall and file countless lawsuits claiming damages from noise pollution, cracks in their homes, in their lives. Driven mad by the constant incoming rush of Boeing jets the residents crack like old plaster. For fifty years people have been moving into the half-priced dwellings surrounding the airport and then clutching their temples and screaming at the skies.

The businessmen come for conventions and stay at the

glass hotels in neatly soundproofed rooms with floor-to-ceiling windows. They stand over half-opened suitcases watching the planes take off and land, a sky full of metal like birds. They never finish unpacking but continue to buy more expensive luggage. They drink in the hotel bars where they meet and run down the day's events, the trade shows, the sales calls. They soak their fingers in jars full of peanuts while they waste the time. They hang their suit coats in the closets. They expense drinks from the wet bar in their rooms and stand with drinks in their hands waiting for the girls they have called from the yellow pages to arrive. They studied business, they were interns, they were born into it. They learned how to sit in strategic negotiations class. They wait for their girls to step from the taxis in black nylons and tiny skirts. They want the girls to look good but they don't want the girls to attract too much attention. They want the girls to look just right. They wait for the girls to show up with suitcases full of leather, studded dildos, whips, candles. They pay extra when the girls hit them. They pay extra when the girls paint their lips. They wait for girls wearing white lingerie with lollipops in their mouths and a bunny tail in the back. The hotel clerks look the other way. Sometimes a girl doesn't look right and some marketing executive sends her packing saying, "No. You are not the one I was promised." He closes his hotel room door on the girl and goes back to his drink and his suitcase by the window with his shirt hanging out of his pants to watch the sky fill with metal.

Brooke has never been turned away but she knows girls who have. Brooke has fat cheeks and big, brown girly eyes. She looks young and thin. She looks like she is a child visiting her father, her many fathers, in hotels surrounding

O'Hare Airport. Most of her fathers live here. Some of them live in cheap motels down on Lincoln Avenue with tractor trailers in the parking lot, but most of her fathers live in the sparkling glass hotels of O'Hare. She always wears black tights or stockings. She always wears a black skirt. She always wears a small black shirt with a silver star in the middle of it whenever she visits her fathers in the hotels.

She runs long fingers along her young face searching for a zit. The taxi speeds next to the trains that run down the middle of the expressway. "So you say you go to the Hilton O'Hare," the driver says to her, drinking in Brooke's crossed legs through the rearview mirror.

"That's right."

"What do you do there," he asks her. "What do you do at the Hilton O'Hare?"

"None of your fucking business." She glances quickly at the driver's ID number, memorizing it. Brooke presses her heels into the taxi's floor and promises herself that she will call the boy the other girl recommended. It's worth paying the extra twenty-five bucks for someone who won't ask dumb questions and will maybe play some rock 'n' roll music during the drive. Someone who will wait for you while you are up in the room on the twelfth floor and guarantee a ride home. The cab driver does not respond, merely drives along, watching Brooke's crossed legs and the road at the same time. He follows Brooke's crossed legs from her ankle to her knee all the way to the Hilton O'Hare.

Brooke steps out of the cab, throws twenty-five dollars at the driver, and flips him the bird. She glides past the doorman without so much as a look. She passes the reception desk, the Andiamo restaurant, and a bright yellow

sports grill advertising steak sandwiches and satellite chan-
nels. She enters the elevator bay and steps out of the elevator
on the ninth floor. She searches in her small black purse for
the scrap of paper. The paper reads 919.

The hotel hallway is an emerald green carpet and a long
series of doors and mirrors. Behind one of the doors a man is
waiting for Brooke. Brooke follows the arrows down the
emerald hall. A large man answers and looks down at Brooke
before stepping aside and letting her in. He has a glass of
scotch with ice in his hand. He still wears brown pants and
a brown jacket with the name tag from some convention ear-
lier. His dark brown hair is cut clean above the roll of his
shoulders. His large belly looks almost muscular pushing
across his belt.

"You must be Madonna," he says to her.

"That's right," she replies. "And you must be Todd even
though your name tag says Mike."

The man blushes for a second. "Whenever I go to a
show, I go as someone else. I don't suppose Madonna is your
real name either."

"It most certainly is."

"You look awful young to be so cocky. Can I fix you a
drink?"

"No thank you."

He takes out his wallet. "Three hundred."

"Yep."

He places the bills in her soft hand and she drops them
casually into her purse.

"My wife died six months ago," he says to Brooke.
Brooke sits in the leather chair next to the bed and the man
sits on the edge of the bed and takes off his jacket and
loosens his tie. "My wife died so now I'm alone."

Brooke leans back in the chair and spreads her legs. "I'm sorry."

"It's all right. We had a good time together. She was a wonderful woman." Brooke checks her watch and the man notices her. While he talks Brooke thinks to herself that he has one hour and no more. She pulls her skirt up gently with the tips of her pinkies. The man talks and talks about his deceased wife. She loses half an hour while he talks. Brooke pulls her skirt all the way up, showing the man her white panties and the top of her pale thighs. When he stops talking Brooke stands on her long legs and moves toward him. She touches his face.

The man stands and takes his clothes off the way he is supposed to. Hookers in Chicago always make Jons in hotel rooms take their clothes off first. It's the only way they know the Jons aren't cops. Brooke rolls a condom over the man's rapidly hardening penis. "Look how big you are," she says. Always compliment them on their size if they have any and their ability if they don't. "You must really do some damage with that thing."

She steps out of her shoes and immediately loses four inches. She unfastens her stockings and throws them next to her purse. She is not worried about her purse or the money. She knows he has money. The hotels at O'Hare are not like those small motels along Lincoln Avenue: the Apache, the Star Deluxe. All of them with cheap bars and live-in tenants. The men in the hotels glittering around O'Hare all have enough money, expense accounts, stipends. Let's have some fun on the company account. Money to burn.

Brooke lays back on the bed and spreads her naked legs. Her skirt falls up over her waist.

"Aren't you going to take off your shirt?"

"That costs extra."

She guides the large man in between her long thin legs. The extra lubricant on the rubber helps. Some guys offer her extra money to do her without a condom but she never takes it. She's not that kind of girl. She relaxes as he pushes into her. She dreams away while holding onto his back. She dreams of a house in Grand Falls, Michigan, and she dreams of shopping and pizza and chocolate shakes.

"Oh yes. Do me like that. Do me just like that, you know exactly how I like it you stud. Do it to me with your enormous cock. Yes."

In five minutes the man comes and Brooke gently pushes him out of her with her hand between her legs making sure the condom stays on. Sometimes you get lucky sometimes you don't. Some clients just stick it in right away and five minutes later you're driving to your next job. Other clients take up half an hour talking about their dead wives, asking you to give them love, to tell them they are special. They pay for a full hour either way so you can't really say no to a little therapy. Still, it sure does bring down the average.

Brooke goes in the bathroom to clean up, bringing her clothes and her purse. She reapplies her makeup, her lipstick. She runs water on a towel and runs the towel between her legs. She kisses the mirror, leaving perfect red marks from her lips. When she comes out the man asks her for her direct number so they can avoid going through the service. He says he would like to see her again and tips her twenty dollars.

The taxis cross through Chicago's knot of highways. The highways are man-made cement rivers and boatmen drive their vessels full of precious cargo. The taxis shuttle through the hotel entrances, running circles past the doormen, circling the night. Brooke walks straight ahead with her sunglasses on, head high. She steps into the first taxi and leans back against the door.

"Maybe we can work out something for a free ride," the cab driver says.

"Dream on," Brooke replies.

3.

ANTHONY LIES in bed staring into the pale green ceiling. He knows the mornings are the price you pay for the night before. When he lies down at night he tries to believe that the morning is going to be better. But he never enters any contests, he doesn't apply for any rewards, and he never gets any letters in the mail. The days rarely change. Sitting up, he is confronted with his own reflection in the enormous mirror he hauled up into his room six months ago.

He stares at his reflection, runs his hand over his face. He stares hard into his eyes, watching himself age. He studies the lines that run past his nose and then turn straight down framing his large red lips. He runs his fingers through his long, golden curls. He looks into his eyes, which are blue. He pulls at the skin on his cheeks. It is a nice face but Anthony hates it. He hates the color of his skin. He hates where his hairline begins. He pulls his hair back behind him and bends forward to examine the top of his head and he hates himself because he is sure he is losing hair.

Anthony lies back in the bed and tries to function within his depression. The clock reads 6 a.m. He has nowhere to be until the evening. He closes his eyes to fall back asleep but it doesn't work. Across from him a maroon phone sits in a cradle. Maybe something will happen tomorrow.

Growing up in Chicago you learn the streets. Chicago is a grid, an easy-to-read map. Any street that intersects Fullerton is 2400 North. That's just the way it is. The city is perfectly flat so distances are easy to measure. Every eight city blocks constitute a mile. If you run from 2400 North to

3600 North, Fullerton to Addison, you have run one mile and a half. You have run from DePaul University, home of the Blue Demons, to Wrigley Field, home of Ernie Banks. On the way you can pass Berlin, the niteclub with black windows underneath the Belmont train station. If you run for ten more blocks to 4600 North you are on Wilson. And if you are on Wilson and Halsted you are in the heart of Uptown, the dark side of Halsted Street.

Uptown has only one industry, the poor. Needle exchanges line Wilson like tiny shopping malls attached to free clinics. Men hide in the corners below the girders, passing the day listening to the music of the trains overhead. Lines of homeless men and women wait outside the various soup kitchens fresh from a night on some thin mattress in an overcrowded homeless shelter. The grown children learn how to huddle beneath the girders on the Elevated Wilson subway tracks. They learn about soup lines and sell bundles beside the long empty windows of Roosevelt University. They live in boarding houses only a mile and a half from the jewel-encrusted trannies stalking the Treasure Island lot. They live in pay-by-the-day hotels when times are bad and beneath garbage bins when times are worse.

Anthony runs along Irving Park toward the lake. The sun has already risen and the population has left for work. 10 a.m. In the late morning Halsted is clean. Shoppers stop at Walgreens on Belmont, at Reckless Records. The restaurant owners wash the come off the sidewalks in front of their stores. He runs past the White Hen on Broadway, then the liquor store and the gas station, breathing white clouds in the cold fall air. His hands are stuffed into a pair of socks. He has a hard time motivating himself to run. He doesn't like it because it is boring and it takes energy. He is not one of those people who claim that running clears their minds. Running does not clear Anthony's mind. He hates to run but he does it almost every morning.

At Lake Michigan Anthony heads north along the trail. Cold crested waves crash onto the beach. The sun spikes through the leaves and along the benches that line the jogging path. The jogging path parallels Lake Shore Drive and goes all the way from Edgewater to the deep South Side. From the jogging path you can see almost every facet of Chicago life. You can see the money steaming off the Gold Coast northeast of the Loop and you can see the smashed-out windows of the project buildings looming over 35th. To the south of Downtown forty blocks of housing projects dot the skyline, a forest of burned-down liquor stores. Chicago is an industrial town, a brick and steel town, a thick, tough town with a glittering landscape of Downtown buildings kissing up against the sky and beach. All of the Downtown buildings rise from its center, beautiful, tall, and strong. Anthony runs away from Downtown. As he runs to the north he passes the ugly condominium complexes, each one cheaper than the one before it the further he runs away. He continues into Rogers Park, Loyola University, and finally the Jonquil Jungle and its tight maze of pawn shops and twenty-four-hour adult bookstores. He stops there at the cemetery placed to keep the city from creeping into the richer suburbs. Anthony grabs his knees for a moment, hears a gunshot, and runs back.

Back in his room he throws his dirty clothes into a card-board box. He does push-ups, sit-ups, chin-ups using a bar he bolted in above the doorframe. He practices dips by moving the chair over by the bed. He needs to sweat. He needs to be stronger.

Anthony steps into the hall wearing a towel. The hall is covered in fuzzy yellow wallpaper with orange patterns running like flames. His feet feel the thin carpet along the floor.

"Anthony!" Mr. Gatskill calls to him. The door to Mr. Gatskill's room is open and the lonely old man sits in a rocking chair. A small mattress lies on his floor and the other half of the room is consumed by an enormous TV playing a game show with the sound turned off. Mr. Gatskill rocks back and forth in the same flannel pajamas he wears every day. He has not worried about how he looks or how he smells in a long time. He lives in his small room on small checks from the government. He has lived in this small room for twenty years. He waves a whiskey bottle toward Anthony. "Have a drink with me."

"No. It's too early. I never drink before five."

"Fuck's sake. Live a little, kid." He hacks into his upturned palm. Once the coughing starts it doesn't stop. Sometimes Anthony hears the coughing late into the night and he is sure the old man is going to die and he will walk into the hallway and see a younger man. A forty-year-old Mr. Gatskill, recently crushed by a bad divorce and the death of his child. He will step into the hall and see a new victim moving in, ready to give up and drink away the rest of his life in this boarding house off of Halsted Street. Anthony watches Mr. Gatskill cough for a few minutes and he watches the amused face of Alex Trebek leading the next round of *Jeopardy* without any sound. Finally Mr. Gatskill catches himself. "Listen, get me a bottle next time you're out," he tells Anthony, clutching the top buttons of his pajamas. "We'll have a drink for my birthday."

"You say that every day."

"Well, why the hell not? What's wrong with birthdays? I

don't know why I even bother with you. You're the meanest young man I ever met in my life." Mr. Gatskill starts coughing again and Anthony walks away.

Anthony moves toward the bathroom and hears the sound of running water. He leans into the wall, arms folded over his naked chest. He waits on the floor's only shower. Eight rooms all share the same shower but it's usually open since no one on this floor has a regular day job. Boarding houses are strange places by most standards and the conventional rules of nine to five, marriage, children, stability, and cleanliness do not apply. The important thing in boarding houses are the televisions and Anthony does not have one so when he wants to watch television he goes to Mr. Gatskill's room.

The door to the shower opens and a black girl Anthony has never seen steps into the hallway. She is soaking wet, wrapped in a towel, her hair dripping and dots of water shining on her dark shoulders. She opens her towel showing Anthony her dark thighs. The towel is too small for her large body anyway. She turns around and then she stops and winks for him. Wink for a sucker. They stare at each other a few moments. A couple of whores on the second floor of a boarding house. Anthony slides past her and into the stall. He wants to get clean.

4.

PEOPLE DANCE for different reasons and at different times. They dance in fading discotheques. They sell themselves to the overhead lights. Some people like it, some people don't, and some people don't have a choice. People sell their time to the giant buildings watching over the lake and all they get is a paycheck in return. People dance at night in various clubs, large and small, to forget their ugly day jobs. They dress in their sexiest clothes, thin black sweaters, tight black pants squeezing their thighs and they make believe they are beautiful. Couples go dancing and wink at each other's partners. Everybody's looking to cheat. Different clubs accommodate different needs. The Crobar forces people to wait in line in the winter even when there is no one inside. Excalibur admits everyone wearing black shoes. People take ecstasy, mushrooms, cocaine, and Special K. People take anything to help them dance.

Anthony places his hands on his hips, and waits for a moment, after the music starts, to whip his shirt to the floor. He glares at the darkness. "Touch me and see what happens." Anthony unbuckles his pants. A hand comes toward him cautiously with a dollar bill. Anthony stamps his foot, just missing someone's fingers, and the hand retreats into the darkness. He immediately regrets it. "Come back," he says, dancing slower, pulling his pants down his well-muscled thighs. He inhales as deeply as he can, beer, sweat, and wood.

People dance for different reasons. "C'mon," Anthony says, pressing his hands against his ribs. He doesn't understand why more people don't come to the stage. Why they only watch him from a distance with drooling eyeballs. He dances for them. He hates them. He longs to be loved by them.

Anthony searches in the light and the film beneath his feet. When he was thirteen Anthony ran away from home. He hung out at a carnival that had set up in the parking lot of the Catholic school. He walked around the roller coaster and the Ferris wheel hawking T-shirts and cotton candy. He worked the bull's-eye game challenging the men walking by to win a stuffed doll for the girl they loved the most. He told the carnies he was eighteen but they didn't care anyway. He lived on a small bed in one of the trucks, setting up in one town and taking down in another. He traveled across America, through the mountains and the desert. The carnival spent a lot of time in Florida and the sick humidity got inside his skin. He traveled with the carnies for over a year, never saying too much. After the shows they opened cans of beer and drank around fires with cans full of chili cooking in the flame. The carnies didn't say too much either. Most of them were missing teeth. Most of them had been in jail. They all had blue tattoos lining their arms and fingers. Some of them were running from something, others had nowhere else to go. At fourteen Anthony liked being a carnie. He liked seeing the country and swearing when he talked. He had never liked school. When the carnival came back to Chicago Anthony walked away without saying anything to the men he had spent the last year with. He walked past the grammar school he had been attending until eighth grade. He walked past the convenience store and the high school he was supposed to be at. He returned home one day after a year, cheeks sunk in his face, wearing a black T-shirt that stated "Circus Fantabulous," and he climbed the steps to the old yellow stucco house. He knocked and waited for his mother's cheap perfume to come to the door and let him in and take him back. It would be like the bad old days. But nobody ever came to the door. His parents had moved. He jimmied open the lock and walked through the empty yellow house staring out the windows to the streets he had grown up on. He knocked on his neighbor's door and the old lady that lived there answered. She explained to him that his parents had moved downstate to Carbondale. She was surprised to see him. Anthony's parents had told everybody that he was living with his grandparents in South Dakota. Anthony told the old lady that he didn't have any grandparents that lived in South Dakota.

After that Anthony became desperate for attention. Slicing open his wrists he walked through the halls of his old grammar school dripping blood waiting for someone to feel sorry for him and to take him home. They didn't. The ambulance came to take him away. The janitor mopped up the floor. People dance for different reasons.

Anthony slides his chest along the lights of the Stolen Pony. He rolls along the floor and stares with big blue eyes toward the bar, the swish of Henry's rag wiping out another glass. The money is not enough. Twice a month he dances on a stage at Berlin, he makes a little more. The Stolen Pony is dimes and tips. The Stolen Pony is a front for boys that suck dick down at the Ram. Anthony doesn't like to suck dick. That is not why he dances.

As the lights go up Anthony rolls off the stage, sweeps the crumpled singles with one hand and, grabbing his belongings with the other, retreats to the back room to change. In the back room he hears shouting from the front. He lowers his face into his hand and tries to keep out the noise. He pulls on his pants. The men in front are hollering for something.

Lance walks up the stage, his long brown braided hair running well past his square shoulders. The men holler for Lance. The lights go down for Lance. Lance spreads his arms for the men. Lance rips his shirt open, whips his belt out of its loops. The men go crazy. Anthony hears Henry say, "This is my kingdom you darling. You will be my prince. We will rule the darkness."

It would be hard to call what Lance does dancing. Lance preens across the stage like a peacock with large, bright feathers exploding off his back. Lance struts across the stage sucking on his cheeks. He puts his hands on his waist and sticks his thin belly out as far as it will go. Lance is sex. He struts back and forth. Everyone wants to own a piece of Lance and Lance licks his lips and laughs and doesn't give a shit about them.

Anthony comes out of the back room fully clothed and sees Lance walking back and forth on the stage, his leather studded underwear grabbing the tops of his thighs, clucking his tongue and waving his crotch at the patrons and the men with shaky fingers who eagerly stuff money in his leather pants for a cheap feel.

Anthony notices Lance's face. The rigid line of his square jaw, the three blue teardrop tattoos dripping below the left eye. Anthony notices the thin muscles of his abdomen, his waist-length brown hair braided like a Norse god's. Anthony sees a girl with dark brown hair and big cheeks watching from a small table by the door, a cigarette balanced on her delicate fingers.

Lance struts for one song and then the lights come on.

The men whistle. Lance bows, his arm brushing the stage floor. Lance gives them a smile just to let them know that everything he owns is for sale, one night only. Anthony stands in the corner with his arms folded across his chest. "Oh honey," Henry gushes. "We love you." Lance moves past Anthony, sneering at him, and into the back room with Henry eagerly following, clutching a contract in his chubby fingers.

Anthony moves toward Brooke seated at the table near the door. "I bought you a whiskey," she tells him and pushes the drink toward him. "All that dancing must make you thirsty."

"Thanks." He sips on his drink.

"I'm Brooke. That was my boyfriend, Lance."

Anthony nods. Looks away.

"I was watching you dance."

"What about your boyfriend?"

"I was watching him dance too. I like it when he dances for me."

"Are you sure he isn't just doing it for the money?"

"A girl can pretend."

Brooke wears an expensive black dress. Anthony touches the fabric of Brooke's dress, rubbing the smooth material between two fingers like an appraiser.

"What's your story, Brooke?" he asks. "What are you doing? How old are you?"

Brooke rolls her eyes at him and, rubbing her ankles together, she downs her drink. "Does somebody care? I didn't realize anybody cared."

"Don't worry about anybody caring. Not in this bar."

"Anthony!" Henry screams. "Get back here."

He steps to the back almost bumping into Lance. "Hey

man," Lance says.

"Hey man yourself," Anthony replies.

There is a moment where the two men meet eyes and drink each other in, wondering who will kill who, before Lance finally smiles and sticks out his hand. "Lance."

They shake hands, eyes locked, as Henry says, "Don't drink on the job. Don't drink whiskey out there. I saw you drinking whiskey with that hooker. I saw you." Henry wags his finger like a jealous lover.

"Who cares about that shit."

"You signed a contract. Also, I expect you to hang out with the patrons between your sets. They like that."

Lance disappears to the front and Anthony stands toe to toe with Henry for a moment before going back out to the front of the bar where he notices the door closing and Brooke alone.

Brooke watches Anthony dance one more set. He does not dance like Lance. He doesn't dance toward the bar. He tries to let the lights of the stage and the music take him somewhere else and when he is done she slides his drink toward him. He sips on it thoughtfully. "Where's your man?"

"He has a date. He'll be back in half an hour."

"Then what?"

"Then we're going to go back home and play Scrabble. Do you want to come?"

Anthony shakes the ice cubes in the glass. At the bar Henry speaks rapidly to a man with a black handlebar mustache.

"Love to," Anthony replies.

Lance walks with a man down Halsted Street. The man holds one hundred dollars in his pocket separate from his wallet. The man wears poorly fitting gray pants. He could work for the Options Exchange, he could be an accountant, he could teach grammar school.

"Have you been in Chicago long?" the man asks quietly.

"I do this all the time," Lance responds.

The boys walking by grab Lance with their eyes, Rough Trade. Lance walks with his head high against the cool breeze and the stranger looks at the ground embarrassed for the obvious. Lance drinks in the smell of suds from all of the bars that leak onto the sidewalk. He holds his chin into the wind. The boys walking by all know and they whisper it with their eyes, Rough Trade. All the world's on glass display on Halsted Street.

They take the steps down below a two-story brownstone. Lance holds open the door and they step inside the Ram's warm air. The books and the videos line the wall, the walls are painted swamp green, and a man with a face like a bear stands behind the glass counter playing solitaire. The man looks up and sees Lance and his Jon and doesn't even smirk. The stranger pushes twenty-five dollars across the counter and a token is packed into his palm. The man could be a father, a bookie, a dealer, a shrink, a salesman, a professor, or a real estate agent. They walk into the theater section of the store, insert token in door, turn knob, step inside.

The stranger touches Lance's hair and takes long, deep breaths. A video plays on a small screen in front of them. The screen waves in blues and greens, naked boys carrying planks of wood with their thin arms on an island. A nudist video, little boy contraband. The man's breath is sour like unwashed hair. The one hundred dollars the man gave Lance sits comfortably in the front pocket of Lance's jeans. Nothing's easier to spend than one hundred dollars from a stranger.

Anthony, Lance, and Brooke walk Belmont without saying much. Lance and Brooke live in the last large building before the expensive condominiums along Sheridan. They live in the last cheap, crappy, undermanaged building before the lake. The hallway entrance to the building is stacked with yellow pages leaning against dark white walls, blocking the doorway. Brooke turns the lock, squeezes the door open as far as it will go into the stacks of yellow pages. An old doorman stands to the side in a ragged blue uniform. The man looks insane, like he has been insane for a long time. Brooke nods to the man but the man doesn't move.

On the wall by the elevator is the list of tenants. There are hundreds.

"What did you get?" Brooke asks.

"One hundred, plus tips from the Pony."

On the thirteenth floor they step into the apartment. Brooke flips a switch and a single, blue, high-watt bulb illuminates an apartment that is beyond filthy. Piles of dirty clothes lie everywhere like miniature mountains in a tiny country. An ironing board stands open but unused in front of a kitchen sink and stove. There is no actual kitchen. There is no bedroom, just an open space filled with clutter. Plastic jewelry sits in a pile with what looks like expensive jewelry. Pieces of a mattress stick out under the piles of clothes and Anthony imagines that would be where they sleep, but if they slept there last night how did so many piles of laundry end up on the bed in just one day? The clutter of their lives has its own energy, moves on its own, consumes and conquers quicker than it can be pushed and cleaned and folded and put away somewhere, put away anywhere. Anthony notices that out the window you can see past the next building to a sliver of lake. A room with a view.

They clear out a space on the floor and Brooke produces the board game from beneath a pair of shoes and plastic skirt. Lance opens the fridge and the yellow light mixes with the blue and then he closes the door and hands Anthony a beer but not Brooke.

"Thanks." They raise their drinks. Brooke sets up the board, the three wooden racks, a bag full of letters. "You're young, Brooke. How old are you?" Anthony asks.

"I'm seventeen. Can you believe it?"

"I can. How long have you been turning tricks?"

"Two years."

"Damn. Fifteen is young for the trade."

"I don't mind it."

"She loves it," Lance says.

"I do love it," she agrees. "The men treat me nice and buy me nice things and I make all this money and it's easy. I just lay back. I don't have to do anything. I give them an hour but usually it takes less. Some of them just want to talk about their wife or some girl that has slighted them. They just want some affection."

"And you give it to them?"

"Oh no. I never give them that. That would be cheating. I only give affection to Lance."

"Her affection is only for me," Lance says, nodding his head.

The three of them spell words into the night, placing the little wooden letters into the grooves, light pink for double, orange for triple. Brooke keeps score on a small white pad. When they finish their beers Lance grabs a couple more. Brooke says, "I love board games."

Lance tries to make up words like ONOUT but Anthony calls him on it. "That's not a word."

"It is a fucking word."

"It's not a word."

"How do you know?"

"I went to college."

Lance stops sipping on his beer; Brooke looks up from her pad. "You went to college?" Lance asks.

"Yeah."

"Where are your college friends?"

"I'm not very good at keeping friends," Anthony explains.

As it gets late Lance brings out a bottle of Jack Daniels and Anthony and Lance pass the bottle back and forth. They start the game over and Brooke spells ZIPPER.

"Holy fuck."

"She always wins."

Anthony nods.

"We met in Grand Falls," Lance says.

"Michigan."

"Yeah. Not much to do in Michigan." Lance spells CUTS.

"Not like Chicago."

"That's for sure."

They stop playing and sit getting more and more drunk. Brooke puts the pieces back in the bag, folds the board, stacks the letter holders, places the game beneath a soft pile near the corner by the window. The darkness of the night threatens to give way to the morning. Lance stops talking. Lance is more beautiful when he is drunk, his sleepy blue eyes lowered toward his cheeks. Brooke sits quietly, wide awake, hugging her legs to her chest. Things could get rough for her one day. Lance has the kind of beauty that will be around for years, that will maybe never go away, unless he has a bad accident. Brooke leans back into the dirty pile and stretches her thin arms over her head.

"He's drunk," Brooke says to Anthony, pointing a finger at Lance who stares intently at the whiskey bottle. "When he gets drunk he gets angry. You better watch out, Anthony."

"Watch out, Anthony," Lance agrees and smiles and for the first time Anthony realizes that Lance might be slightly mad. He drinks them in, Lance sitting quietly staring into a bottle of whiskey as if there was a boat inside it and Brooke with her arms spread, her shaved armpits displayed, leaning against the dirty clothes for support.

"I better stumble my ass on home," Anthony says.

"Guess you best."

Past the stacks of yellow pages in the hallway the doorman is still in attendance. He nods toward Anthony, the keeper of the dawn.

Anthony stops in the Lakewood and picks up a pint of whiskey for Mr. Gatskill. He walks up the stairs half drunk from his long night. He sees Mr. Gatskill asleep in his chair and pulls the empty bottle out of his hand and replaces it with the full one.

In his room Anthony strips down and stares at the mirror leaning against his wall. He sucks in his cheeks, turns his body. He is not well hung. The room spins slightly, the mirror stays in place. He lays down on the floor, pushes himself, his nose touching the mirror then pulling back an inch.

Anthony stares at the mirror and pushes himself up on his arms. He lowers himself again, Lance's whiskey still moves through his stomach. He pushes himself up and lowers himself and pushes himself up and lowers himself and up again and his stomach tightens. He does as many push-

ups as he can. He does push-ups until he throws up splat-
tering his mirror and his floor.

5

INDIAN SUMMER. Every November there is a week that is unseasonably warm in Chicago. The people flock outside. They bicycle along the beachfront. The kids play basketball on the schoolyard courts. The ones that are really good play basketball at the court on Foster Beach where professional scouts hang out trying to get a whiff of the next big thing. When the children dive to the rim, their entire bodies extend toward the hoop and the bright orange ball an extension of that and the sun an extension of the bright orange ball. The kids scream and thump their chests and raise their hands toward the lake daring it to take them away. Every year somebody makes it off that court into a Big Ten college. Every year someone gets carried away on a white stretcher, their blood spilled, stained, and left on the basketball court at Foster. The scouts try to duck when the bullets start flying and boys fly to the rim during Indian Summer.

Brooke and Lance sit outside of Caribou Coffee in the morning with paper cups full of coffee sitting in front of them on the faux-wood tables. Next to each coffee is a pager. From where they sit they can see the Treasure Island supermarket and the shoppers leaving the store with fancy paper bags full of fresh vegetables and imported jars of special fish. The paper bags have handles and pictures of movie stars. It's part of the experience.

Brooke and Lance hide behind their sunglasses. It's early and Lance doesn't like to be up. Last night they went to the Smart Bar. The bouncer lifted the rope for them. The bartender comped them a drink. Brooke and Lance are good for business. The manager treated them to a line of cocaine in the plush VIP booth away from the stage where a bouncer stood holding a velvet rope. Lance still feels high-strung. Cocaine wrings him dry and makes him feel tight. He knows the drugs will irritate him. He knows he has bad sides, sides that are jagged, angry, and unpredictable. But he never says no. He always says yes.

Brooke likes a little cocaine once in a while. She likes to have a good time, she likes to dance, she likes to wear sexy clothes. She likes the niteclubs. Now she looks at Lance lovingly from behind her sunglasses. He is every seventeen-year-old girl's dream. He is so alternative, so good-looking. He's ten years older than her. He has experience.

"I'm going to enroll in modeling school," she says, making up her mind. "I'm going to be a model."

"Good idea."

"I could be a model. I have nice eyes and long legs."

Lance reaches under the table and grabs her leg. "You do have good legs. I could scarf you up right now."

Brooke blushes and pushes Lance away. Their two pagers sit on the table next to their cups of coffee and the sun washes over both of them while the table starts rattling. They look at the table together. It's Brooke's pager jumping up and down next to her coffee. She picks up her coffee and takes a sip before grabbing the jumping pager to check the number.

"I have a call."

"I can see that." Lance is keenly aware of the discrepancy in their incomes. Sometimes Brooke makes one thousand dollars in a day. Lance is lucky if he can make a hundred. Brooke won't give Lance any of her money. She says you have to earn your money. That's what her daddy taught her.

Her daddy the lawyer told her that people need to make their own money. He told her she should never give money to poor people because poor people are lazy scum who don't know how to work. Her daddy told her that they should go into the projects and force all of the homeless people to have surgery to prevent them from having any more welfare babies. Her daddy told her that people need to make their own money. He told her money is important. Brooke never shares her money with Lance.

Lance sips his coffee and Brooke gets up to use the pay-phone on the corner. A car stops in the street to let some kids cross and then another car pulls up behind it. The car in back honks loudly at the stopped car and the kids run laughing to the other side. The car honks loudly again and the coffee pours into Lance's veins which squeeze through his body, crowded into his muscles by all of the people walking the streets for Indian Summer. The streets are filled with sun and the musical accompaniment of the screeching horn. Lance stands and whips his coffee cup at the offending car and the coffee explodes against the windshield. The coffee flies out of the cup and coats the windshield and rains down on the roof, and the paper cup rolls down the hood and lands on the pavement. The horn stops, people stare, Brooke finishes her call.

Tommy leans against the glass of the donut shop, sleep-less and hungry. Last night he slept in a broom closet in the entryway to a three flat. He's an ugly kid, with a bumpy, uneven face. Other kids sit near Tommy spitting and smoking and saying witty things to people passing by. They are used to being ignored. It's their way of life. Tommy won't go home tonight, or the night after. Tommy spies Anthony in sweatpants and turns to his friend and says, "Dare me?" And his friend shrugs his shoulders and laughs. "Hey give me a dollar," Tommy says to Anthony, who is walking home from a long run along the lake. Anthony stops for a moment, his lips forming a cruel sneer. Anthony places his fists against his waist and Tommy backs up an inch. The kids don't usually ask Anthony for money. They don't bother the locals. Instead, they hit up the shoppers and the newbies, hoping to hit someone who hasn't been hit before.

"No," Anthony says.

"I see you going into that fag club," Tommy's friend says.

Anthony ignores Tommy's friend and considers what to do. "I'll tell you what," Anthony says, looking down at Tommy, taking in the boy's young, mean features. "I'll give you a dollar if you never ask me for anything ever again."

"Deal," Tommy says.

"I don't want to know you. Don't ever talk to me. Don't even look at me."

"Nothing to look at."

Anthony reaches into his jacket pocket and pulls out a crumpled single which he tosses onto Tommy's knee and it rolls into his lap.

"Don't touch it," the other kid says. "You don't know where it's been."

Tommy takes the dollar, stretches it out then folds it into his pocket. He turns his attention from Anthony to his side. Anthony stays standing over him. "Hey, give me a dollar," Tommy says to a young man in a long wool coat. Tommy sucks on his lips then turns back to Anthony. "What are you hanging around for?" he asks.

"You're not very likeable," Anthony tells him.

"You're not either," Tommy replies.

"Are you a gigolo?" Tommy's friend asks. "You ever suck a guy off for money?"

"Why, you looking to get into the business?"

"You don't have any chance," Anthony says to Tommy. "You're fucked. Nobody's going to help you." Tommy fingers the bill in his pocket and decides he will buy cigarettes with it. Anthony looks from Tommy to his friend. "Your friends are going to leave you behind," Anthony says. "They're not even going to turn you over in the bed when you start to vomit in your sleep." Tommy wears discarded clothes, the kind people give away. His friend wears a beat-down black jacket and jeans that are intentionally torn. His friend has blue hair. Hair dye costs money. "You're gonna die on these streets and nobody's going to give a damn, either."

"You oughta get out of here," Tommy says.

"You *oughta* have better manners when somebody gives you a buck. I've been here longer than you. I don't *oughta* go anywhere." Tommy looks to his side to see one of the girls coming up and Anthony unballs his fists and walks away.

"Who was that?" she asks.

"A sucker," Tommy replies.

Anthony turns on the light in his room, takes off his shoes, pulls off his socks and replaces them with a clean pair. Very few people have ever been in Anthony's room. Mr. Gatskill comes over sometimes but usually Anthony goes over to his room because he has the television. Also, Mr. Gatskill smells bad and Anthony doesn't want his room to smell like Mr. Gatskill. Anthony's room is not large, but it is clean.

Once Anthony brought home a transvestite prostitute he picked up in front of the Vortex. There was also Jane, who used to live in his building. Jane came in one day wearing blue jeans with snakeskin boots. She said she was from Texas and had come to make it in the big city. Anthony pointed out that she was in the wrong big city, that she probably wanted to go to New York or Los Angeles where they made lots of films but Jane disagreed with him. She said Chicago was definitely the city she had meant to go to and that she was going to make it here. She came into Anthony's room a few times and they had something that resembled a relationship. Jane would walk into Anthony's room and start taking her clothes off. Anthony would turn off the lights because he didn't want to see the blue veins in her legs. Then she would lie down on his bed and he would pull his pants down to his knees and enter her. When they had sex Jane would talk to him about all of her favorite movies. She would tell him how she loved the old movies the best, *Casablanca*, *The Maltese Falcon*, *It's a Wonderful Life*. She would list all of the reasons she was going to be a great actress. She said she knew how to cry. She said she could pretend to be in love with anybody. She said she had been acting all of her life. Sometimes she would quote some line from the Shakespeare book she kept in her room and she would say it with an English accent.

"That's how you do it," she would say.

"Yeah, great," Anthony would reply as he pushed in and out of her. "I'm sure you'll make it big." Sex for them was the same as having coffee. There was no passion. It was just an excuse to make conversation.

Jane started to bring home other men. She would give Anthony the signal if he saw her in the hall with them. The signal meant that he should pretend not to know her and not say anything at all. That was easy enough for Anthony. But Anthony didn't like the men she brought home. Obvious

con men, phonies in bad polyester. They wore fake gold
chains and smelled of cheap restaurants. She would come
into his room and tell him how she had gotten a part in some
play or how somebody was going to make a movie out of her.

"He said I have a star quality."

After a while Anthony refused to have sex with her anymore. He didn't want to be part of the pile of men that she
brought home. If the men she brought home had been beautiful, if they had all looked like Lance, then he wouldn't
have minded. But he didn't want to be part of an ongoing
parade of lies, bad skin, and tight-shouldered suit jackets.
Jane didn't care anyway. Their relationship continued on
exactly the same. They would just talk in Anthony's room
with the lights off. She always led the conversation. She
always told him about her acting career. It never sounded
very good.

One day Jane was gone. In boarding houses people come
and go. There is little personal investment. There is no
reason to stay except the reason of having nowhere else.
Anthony presumed Jane had gone back to her family in
Texas after she finally realized that she was never going to
make it as an actress.

Mr. Gatskill told Anthony he read about Jane in the
Chicago Sun Times. He said a blonde-haired girl was killed
down on 18th and Taylor. "She was killed by the coons!" Mr.
Gatskill said thumping his palms against the arms of his
chair. "Killed. I recognized her from the photograph."

"You're full of shit," Anthony told him. "She went back
to Texas to be with her family."

"How do you know? How do you know!?"

"Because," Anthony lied. "She sent me a letter."

"A letter?"

"Yeah. She sent me a letter. It said she had made a mistake in coming to Chicago and she was going to work on her family's ranch raising cattle."

"A letter. You get letters?"

"I get letters all the time."

Anthony's room is not a very large space and it grew smaller after Jane left. Very few people have ever seen the inside of it.

6

FOX WIPES down the bar at Berlin. She stacks the bottles in back. She connects the kegs to the taps. She makes sure there are enough bottles of water in the cooler. The water costs three dollars and the door costs ten but the space is free. The kids come in and they take X or K and they just want to drink water and pop pills all night. Nobody likes to feel bad in the mornings. Nobody should ever wake up in the morning and feel like they made a mistake. Fox looks for smudges on the mirrors, the video monitors, the DJ booth.

Fox makes sure everything is OK. People say she is the most powerful person in the Chicago Underground. Other people wonder if the Chicago Underground really exists. Berlin lies below the Belmont train station and its dark black window foreshadows nothing of what's inside. Every night there's a crowd and the people inside don't know what is there. A person could walk through the crowd and hear some music, see video screens playing, kids dancing with necklaces. They would see strippers on the stage or a woman dancing with fire, but they would not really know what is inside. Nobody knows the first time, but they keep coming back. The kids come back to Berlin because the kids are addicted to Berlin. It is not the drugs that they do, or the drinks, or even the dancing. They are addicted to the club and never stop to question why. Fox manages Berlin. She appraises the boys that are going to dance on the stage. She has final say on the door. She knows who's a dealer and who's a cop. She brings in the dominatrices with their ropes and whips and racks. She picks the music and she dances while she checks over the bars. She dances in the club alone with the sound speakers playing exactly what she wants to hear, with her arms spinning over her head and her red hair flying above her shoulders.

Fox has long legs and long red hair. She wears blue jeans. People say she is conservative looking for a niteclub manager. She wears small earrings, glasses with thin frames and light sweaters. People say she is pretty. People say she is beautiful. They say she is stiff, unattractive. People always say things about Fox. She is the talk of the town. They say she has never been in love, that she is as cold as the winter. They say she made a bad decision years ago and has been lonely ever since.

Fox hires bouncers, bartenders, lets kids in free if they're early and they're good dancers. She knows who all the good dancers are. She knows everything. She runs Berlin and passes on the profits to nameless owners and bankers that come in with metal briefcases. She is the glue that holds it all together. There are bartenders that make more than her. Like Toni who works the best bar every Thursday, Friday, and Saturday and is voted the best bartender every year in *NewCity*, the official unofficial magazine of nothing. She doesn't worry about money, she makes enough. She holds a thin thread of power, it could be cut anytime, and it would all go with her, not the building, not the children, just all of it. She dances across a precarious tightrope suspended over a mythical underground, an imaginary kingdom, and the police push and the owners push and the bankers push and the mayor pushes and the kids dance and take drugs and parade on top of a secret that everybody knows, but nobody's telling. And they all talk about Fox.

A large white limo holds the curb in front of Berlin. Two men with thick arms in long coats stand in front of the car blowing into their hands. Anthony passes them. It is a long car. Clean. Anthony feels his pocket and worries that he's running short on cash.

It's almost midnight. Anthony waves to Fox and heads downstairs below the coatcheck to wait for the music to stop. The man will soon call, "Time for your set." In front of him a stripper named Michael does push-ups on the floor. Anthony watches Michael's back as the muscles ripple in waves across his wide, dark shoulders.

A girl walks past them wearing a catsuit with patterns of a cheetah and six-inch stiletto heels. The girl has just come from the stage where she took volunteers from the audience and handcuffed them to a crucifix and flogged them with a whip. She smirks at Anthony and Michael. She stops and turns to them. "What is art?" she says. "We are performance." And then she walks away.

Berlin sits under the Belmont train tracks. Half of the trains in Chicago converge at Belmont and Halsted. The Ravenswood, also known as the brown line, stops there coming from Kimball on its way to the Loop. The old North South, also known as the red line, passes through from Howard on its way to 63rd and University deep on the South Side. In the mornings and after work the Evanston Express, also known as the purple line, makes one of only two stops before Downtown at Belmont. For Chicago, all of the world converges at Belmont. Below Chicago is Berlin. The doors never open before ten at night. Berlin's windows are darkened to protect the sweaty bodies crushed together from the gawkers walking the street, from the people that don't know and from the people that can't get in. The bodies in Berlin sweat piles of pills and powder. The bathrooms cut lines of cocaine and pass aspirin bottles of ecstasy for twenty-five dollars a pop. There is always a show at Berlin and twice a month or more Anthony is part of that show for one hundred dollars and as much as he wants to drink from the bar.

Anthony hasn't danced in two days and feels desperately empty. The call comes and Anthony leaves Michael still pounding away at the floor and the cheetah girl now half undressed, her breasts sagging without the support of her suit, looking lonely near the deep green walls. He climbs to the stage and looks across the heads and grabs onto the wooden apparatus with its chains and wrist clamps and pushes himself against it. He loops an arm over the cross and as the music picks up he picks up as well.

A woman comes to the stage with some money and he leans down to take it from her and he gets on his belly so his face is next to hers and he kisses her lips hoping to feel something. Her husband rubs the dollar bills on Anthony's back and the money falls off of him as he pushes himself away.

The back of the stage is lined with mirrors and he dances with himself. The music in Berlin is louder than his thoughts. Fox watches it all from behind the bar. He sits on the edge of the stage and hands reach across his legs. He can't see out into the bar, he can only feel the hands stretching up his naked legs and the arms pulling him from the stage, running up his thighs like strong wind. He hears whispers in the music. He feels the whispers in the fingers slipping into the band of his underwear. He has to pull away. He has to take himself back. Anthony knows the rules. He crawls away from the edge. He crawls toward the mirror and as the third song plays he makes his way to the basement.

Dressed, Anthony orders a whiskey with ice from the bar, and Fox hands it to him without saying a word. A man in sunglasses approaches.

"That's my limo out front," he says by way of introduction. "You like limousines?"

"I don't live too far away," Anthony says. "So I've never found one necessary."

The man pulls a bill out and with two fingers pushes it down the front of Anthony's pants. "I own a limousine company," he says. "We're going to make a commercial. If you would learn how to smile we could put you in it. Dress you up like a chauffeur. We're going to advertise in all the gay magazines too." He leans forward with a sheepish grin like someone who thinks he is attractive but isn't.

Anthony sips on his drink and pulls a pen and pad from the bar and writes down a number. Turns the pad over.

"Why don't you come over," the man says to Anthony. "It'll just be you and me. We can talk about your future. I'll have the servant make fish. Do you like fish?"

"Just you and me?" Anthony says. "Doesn't sound very fulfilling." Anthony gives the man a look, turning his head toward him, over his shoulder, his body still facing the stage. The man is thin. He has a crooked nose that fits his face perfectly. His neck is bent forward, his posture is like a question mark.

Maybe when I was twenty, Anthony thinks. A young sucker chasing every lead. He remembers dancing naked for a play Downtown. He remembers some parties around a pool, old men and fancy drinks. He didn't have to get wet too many times to figure it out. The worst of it is that they think for a few dollars you will love them back.

"Can I buy you another drink," Limousine Man asks

while simultaneously calling the bartender. The bartender looks at Anthony who always drinks free and Anthony says, "I'll take the most expensive thing you have."

When the drinks arrive the two men touch glasses. Anthony pulls the bill out of his pants and turns over the pad he wrote on. The pad reads, *One Dollar*.

"Look," Anthony says. "They match."

"There's more where that came from. Lots more."

"Why don't you find somebody like yourself," Anthony says, looking away, touching his elbows to the bar. "Find someone that looks like you if there's nothing wrong with it."

The man's posture tightens, like a grape drying into a raisin. Anthony picks up his drink and his dollar and walks away.

Brooke stands next to the emergency exit in the narrow corridor blocking Anthony's way. "You were good tonight," Brooke says, wrapping her lips around a red straw. In her hand she holds a bright blue cocktail. "Who's your friend?"

"You're too young to be in here," Anthony tells her, taking a drink from his own glass, then another.

"I'm too young to be in anywhere, Anthony."

The cheetah girl returns to the stage, her confidence back, in full uniform. She cracks her whip. She bends down to her knees and points a finger at the crowd of dancers. She runs her tongue across her whip.

"I like the way you dance."

"You like watching men strip."

"Most strippers can't dance. Most dancers don't strip. You're a dancer."

"You should leave here, Brooke. This is no place for you."

"You've got me wrong. I'm a niteclub girl. I live for the clubs, to dance. Don't you want to dance with me?"

"No. I'd rather dance toward you."

"Look," Brooke nods to the stage. "She wants you." The cheetah girl is staring right at Anthony with one foot planted in front of the other.

"Fuck that. I work here."

"Don't be so removed," Brooke tells him and pulls him with her toward the stage. The sea of people part for them. A seventeen-year-old hooker and a damaged stripper, niteclub royalty. VIPs in a secret nation run by show promoters and niteclub owners. The bartenders are their lieutenants, the doormen soldiers on the line. At the stage Brooke hands him over. The Cheetah pulls off his shirt and runs her claws across him. She binds him to the wooden cross. "Put a blindfold on him," Brooke shouts. "He's shy." The Cheetah covers his eyes, pushes her body into his, hard. Her suit makes her perfect and Anthony tries to block out the image of her in the dressing room, lonely, with one sagging breast hanging from her expensive outfit. He imagines a cat, strong and fast, its fur wrapping around him, her tail around his neck. Other fingers, other voices. He wonders if they belong to Brooke. Long fingers, thin fingers, tracing him. Then the fingers are gone and it is dark with music. The straps start to hit him. They don't hurt so much. They sting slightly. The straps come more frequently and he loses himself in the pain. Then they stop, and a hand smacks him across the face. The warm body follows. "Everything is going to be OK," the body says. But Anthony knows better.

Brooke takes one last look at Anthony from the door. He has a perfect body, better even than Lance. Every line on his body intentional. Every muscle built and placed on purpose. He has a manufactured body, smooth and shaven, symmetrical. She takes a last look at the body that Anthony has built. Anthony's project. Not like Lance. Lance never works out, drinks all the time, eats pizza. Lance has a line of hair from his belly button that he doesn't worry about. Poor Anthony, he has to work so hard. The cheetah lady has pulled more people on stage, men and women, and they all rub their hands over the body that Anthony has built. Poor Anthony up on stage in the dark and all of the strangers washing over him.

The door closes behind her and she pulls her jacket close. As Indian Summer ends the winter is going to come in, she just knows it. The cold is going to smash over the rocks at Belmont Beach.

Brooke walks down Belmont toward her home. The nights love Brooke. They love her shiny black outfits, her long thin legs. Tommy and other kids in front of Dunkin' Donuts tuck in their feet when she walks by. She makes too much to sit with the runaways. The men that huddle in the corners don't follow her waiting for a chance. The hookers don't hiss, "Mamacita baby girl."

Brooke thinks back to Grand Falls, Michigan. She lived in a blue bedroom and slept on a four-post bed. The maids kept her company. The maids cleaned her room, cleaned the house, cleaned the things she would drop on the floor. There were so many maids. Her mother took pills to kill the time and her father worked long hours. When her father came home to their house with all of its rooms and all of the maids he would talk to Brooke. He would tell her about his work. He was a stern man. He didn't drink or smoke. He ate salads and exercised. He was tall and handsome and her mother was getting fatter every year and losing her mind. Her father would sit at the table with Brooke and tell her what he thought was true. That the only thing that matters in this world is money. That money is the only thing that can keep you safe. That without money you are like a fish without water. You will starve, you will suffocate, you will drown. You will flip and flop smacking your tail into the ground. But her father was not bothered by her excesses. Brooke spent money. She bought anything that looked interesting just to fight off the boredom. Her walls were lined with thousands of tapes and CDs. She was always bored when her father was not around. She pined for him. And when Daddy was home they would talk and he would tease her, "When you are older, when your mother is gone, you can be my girlfriend."

But her mother was never gone. And he didn't mean it anyway, it was just a joke they had. She never became her daddy's girlfriend. She got too bored. She hated school. She left Grand Falls to get some kicks in Chicago. But she'd go back one day. She just wanted to give her mother enough time to leave or to die. She wanted her mother to get tired of her father's infidelities and go. Then Brooke would go back home.

Closer to the lake the wind cuts her face. She crosses through the tunnels under Lake Shore Drive and comes up on the beach and feels the splash of wet air. The beach late at night is dark except for lights from the cop cars searching the fresh graffitti on the rocks and the trees. Nobody rides down the bicycle path late at night.

Brooke skirts the cop cars easily, ducking the beams of light, steps down the rocks toward the water. The waves splash against the large grey stones, twisted in sharp angles, plowed to the shore. Down the lake Navy Pier sticks out into the water. The enormous Ferris wheel, much celebrated, stands all lit up, not moving. Brooke will ask Lance to go for a ride on the Ferris wheel. She pulls off her long black boots. She peels down her tights and throws them on the rocks. She dips her toes in the water. She looks for her daddy in the stars. She sings lightly and calls to the lake. She hums for boats and tries to pull them toward the rocks.

Back home Brooke enters her enormous building. Opening the door to her apartment she sees dark piles of dirty clothes and hears Lance sleeping somewhere in the mess. Sliding along the clothes she feels for Lance's back, runs her fingers along his spine. He shakes, tries to get her to leave him alone. She kisses the back of his neck. He turns over and grabs her and she smells the night's drinks on his breath. He grabs her legs.

"Where's your panties?"

"I left them on the rocks at the lake."

"You're a whore. That's all you are."

"I am. I'm your whore."

Lance pulls her skirt up. Brooke wraps her hands across his shoulders. Lance pushes into her and because it is so dark and so filthy in the room Lance cannot see her thinking of Anthony tied to the rack at Berlin. She holds him as close as she can and cries as he pushes into her again and again. She begs him not to stop. She wishes she still had a maid around to clean up the mess.

It never stopped. Berlin closed, the burly bouncers came through with sticks and crowded the dancers, the drug users, the kids dressed in black, the tattooed, the pierced, the angry and the beautiful out onto the street through the one tiny door. Every night it takes forever. Every night Berlin has to close or the real bouncers in Chicago will come, the Chicago Police with their cars and their guns. Their sticks are bigger, there are more of them, they have more power, they have unions, blue shirts and badges. The police are backed by the politicians, the army, the national guard, the FBI, the US Reserve. But as long as the bouncers push everyone out and the owners pay the right people the right amount, which is the way business has always been done in Chicago, then the real bullies never come, and the clubs and the nights exist for themselves and forever.

Now the club is empty, except for one large bouncer named Colin sitting on a stool by the door with enormous wooden earrings pushing open his ears so his lobes brush his shoulders. Colin's got his own problems. His arms are covered with thick black tattoos and he speaks with Fox who silently counts the money from the door without even looking to the stage. The last bartender wipes down the bar and stacks up the bottles and lifts the slats. The bartender is rich again. The bartenders at Berlin never hurt for cash. All of the lights are on and the floor is filled with spilled cocktails. And on the stage Anthony is still tied to a cross and a woman in a cheetah suit still plays with him but now she only touches him gently. Across his chest are red marks. His back bleeds from her nails. She touches Anthony's chest. She runs her hand over his face. Tears flow from beneath his blindfold and run down his cheek but his mouth doesn't move. She kisses his wet cheeks. She holds his body closely against hers because she knows he will not go home with her. When the blindfold comes off the tears will stop and he will be gone like all of the men she has brought on the stage before. She holds his body closely for comfort, feels the heat from his chest and his arms strain against their bindings. She kisses him and his mouth opens and their tongues intertwine in the darkness of the empty niteclub with all of the lights turned on.

7

BEFORE LANCE leaves for his stint at the Stolen Pony he turns a trick at a cheap hotel. Before Lance shows up at the Stolen Pony he hangs out on a street corner trying to get a lift in a fancy car. Before Lance shows up at the Stolen Pony he robs Brooke while she's sleeping. He pulls the blanket off of her to watch her sleep naked while he robs her. He sticks his hand in her little black purse and opens it quietly while the moonlight glows on her pale, naked back. He watches the soft movements of her lips in her sleep. He feels the walls of her purse and he pulls out the heaping pile of tens, twenties, and fifties she keeps there. The money she finds on the floors at hotels out by O'Hare Airport. He counts out what he thinks she won't notice. He watches her legs. He watches her toes. Her body is clean. Her skin is tight, smooth, and young. Lance loves Brooke but he steals from her because she is so cheap. She will never give him anything. And she makes so much money and doesn't spend it on anything except new clothes which she wears once and then throws on the floor. She never shares her money. Brooke breathes softly while he robs her and her soft breathing circles through the room. He watches her stomach. He pushes the money into the pocket of his jeans and thinks to himself that he will try his best not to hurt her. He gently pulls the blanket back over Brooke's naked, sleeping body.

Lance enters the Pony as the first snow of the year falls. Lance is almost hit by a snowflake before walking through the door. Anthony is already there, wearing tight jeans and a wifebeater, standing at the bar next to a bulldog-faced man with short black hair. The man tells Anthony how he raises dogs and sells them. "It's like selling people," the man says. "Only it's dogs, so it's legal."

Anthony scratches his chest. Anthony doesn't respond to the man just stands with him fulfilling Henry's requirement of standing at the bar between sets. Anthony nods to Lance and Lance goes into the back room to change. There are only eight men in the bar.

Lance comes out to dance when the music starts. He walks back and forth on the stage and the men come to him, even the man who looks like the dogs he raises and then sells, leaves Anthony to join the other men standing close by the stage. While Lance is hustling for tips Anthony is getting bored and when Lance is done Anthony takes his place, but while Anthony dances the men stare from a distance and the distance makes Anthony angry. Between sets Anthony goes into the back room and sits on an empty keg of beer and opens a newspaper.

"You get out there and socialize," Henry says with his arms at his hips. "You know the rules."

Anthony looks up at Henry and thinks he is a fat fucking queen. "I'm not feeling sociable."

"Then clean out some beer glasses."

"You got me confused with someone else." Anthony turns the pages of the newspaper.

"Maybe you want to go home for the day," Henry scolds Anthony like a schoolteacher. Anthony lays his newspaper down next to him.

"Maybe you want to suck my dick you fat fuck."

Lance enters the back room. Henry glows when he sees Lance's face. "Why can't you be more like Lance? Why do you have to be so violent?"

"Yeah. You should be more like me, Anthony. Less violent." Lance adopts a stance with one leg back, his hand behind his belt as if he had a knife and was ready to use it.

Anthony looks up at Lance's smiling face. He knows Lance. He has seen men like Lance come through the boarding house. Men fresh from jail or the nut bin, the kind that always go right back. Some inherent deficiency that makes them capable of anything. Anthony smiles back at Lance because Anthony is not afraid of men like Lance. At least they are predictable. Anthony would trade everything he has ever had to be beautiful the way that Lance is beautiful. The way that Lance is beautiful is the way that is always beautiful. Beautiful as a child and beautiful as an old man. People have always loved Lance for his beauty, spoiled him with their love and affection, so much so that now Lance doesn't care at all. It's a way that doesn't care, that has beauty in spite of itself, at least in Anthony's eyes. At least the way Anthony sees beauty.

"Why don't you come back to my place tonight and let's get drunk."

"Why the hell not," Anthony agrees.

Henry not wanting to take things any further retreats to the bar and the music starts up and Anthony begins to prepare himself for his next set. He does push-ups on the floor, then sit-ups.

"Look at you," Lance says.

"Look at yourself," Anthony replies.

They enter the apartment. The piles of clothes have gotten higher. The clothes are consuming the apartment. Lance tosses a beer at Anthony and Anthony catches it just before it smacks him in the face. Anthony sits on a pile of clothes and opens his beer and Lance sits on another pile across from him like two kings sitting on their thrones discussing the fate of the world just before the Germans drop the bombs.

"So you dance at Berlin. How is that?"

"It's a good job. There's more people than the Pony. You make a little bit more money and it smells better."

Lance stands up and moves toward Anthony. He turns so Anthony can see his leg and his shoulder. "Do you think they have work for me there?"

"I'm sure there's work for you everywhere."

"You think things are easy for me but I've seen some times," Lance tells him. "I've seen some things. I've done some time."

"I know about teardrops," Anthony replies and Lance strokes the teardrops tattooed down his own face.

"I got framed when I was younger for stealing a car. They put me in jail for four years."

"That's a long time for a first offense," Anthony says.

"It wasn't my first offense."

Anthony watches Lance standing in front of him. Lance wants to tell him something but doesn't know what it is he wants to say. He looks at the ceiling then stares back at Anthony and lets out a low growl then sits back down and they sit quietly, contemplating their beers.

Lance has a ritual, a simple one. He drinks beer, then he drinks whiskey. Lance finds a pint bottle buried in a pile of clothes.

"Like looking for a needle in a haystack."

"How long do you think it would take to fall from the window of this apartment?" Lance asks. Anthony shrugs his shoulders. Lance grabs an empty beer bottle, opens the window and casually drops it. There is silence and then there is a crash. Lance takes another bottle and whips it toward the alley and there is a louder crash and it comes quicker. Then there is shouting. A man screams from the street that Lance should not throw any more bottles and then there is more crashing as Lance responds with every bottle he can find that is empty in the filthy apartment and the man hides under an archway from the hail of glass.

"I guess that's how long," Anthony says.

Lance pushes his hand into the wall then sits down with his whiskey looking restless. They wait. "Come here," Lance says. Cold swirls in the apartment through the open window and Anthony gets up to leave.

"You're leaving me. My girl is not even home and you're going." Lance takes off his shirt and begins to unbuckle his pants.

"I'm not good with people," Anthony replies and opens the door. The door and the window create a tunnel and a cool wind blows harshly through the apartment. Anthony pulls the door shut behind him and walks to the elevator. As the elevator door opens he is faced with three policemen and the policemen push him back against the wall and put a baton to his throat.

"You're not going anywhere, buddy." The cops grab Anthony and drag him down the hall to Lance's apartment. One cop kicks in Lance's door and the latch pops off and falls to the floor. Lance looks up from his throne. "Jesus Christ," the cop says staring across the apartment, amazed by the piles of clothes, the dirt on the walls, and Lance sitting on a pile of laundry in his underwear, his eyes bloodshot and downcast. "Put your clothes on. You're gonna sweep some glass, kid."

The other cop turns to Anthony, the cop's belly bulging over a thick black belt. "And what about you?"

"I don't even know this guy," Anthony says.

"He doesn't even know me," Lance agrees.

The cop lets go of Anthony and Anthony rubs his throat and walks away staring back down the hall at the cops waiting for Lance to get dressed. He rides the elevator down. The elevator opens on the ground floor and Brooke steps in.

"Don't go up there," Anthony says. "The cops are up there."

"What did he do?"

"He just broke some glass. No big deal."

The elevator starts to rise and Brooke stops it between floors.

"You're just a girl, Brooke. What do you think you're going to do?"

She runs a finger over Anthony's face, tracing the lines, making sure they are real. "Did you make this line?" she asks. "Or was it always there?" He doesn't respond. "It's such a pretty line." She pushes her finger along his cheek. And then she presses the button to get off on the next floor. They get off the elevator and she says to Anthony, "What are they going to do to Lance?"

"What did they do last time?" he responds.

"Meet me tomorrow," she says. "Meet me in the morning."

"Why would I do that?"

"We need to talk."

They are on the second floor and it is the same as the floor Brooke lives on with Lance, dirty, unattended.

"You know what would happen if they cleaned these walls?" Anthony says running a finger along the border and pulling it away with a thick pile of dust on the tip. "They'd raise the rent. Then they'd kick you out. You and Lance."

"Don't be a jerk. Nobody likes a jerk."

Anthony taps his foot. "All right. I'll meet you. I'll meet you at the school."

"No, meet me at the diner on Melrose."

"I don't like food," he tells her.

"Don't starve me," she tells him. "Do something nice. It's good for you."

"Where'd you hear that? The Saturday morning cartoons?"

"I'm not as young as you think I am."

"You're seventeen."

"I'm seventeen."

"That's how young I think you are."

Brooke gets back in the elevator and Anthony walks down the stairwell. Leaving the building he sees Lance with a broom and a dustbin sweeping the pavement while three of Chicago's finest stand around him like lions deciding how they are going to eat a freshly killed gazelle.

8

IT'S LONG past dark and the Lakewood is lit up in bright red lights. Anthony doesn't mind having a drink in the Lakewood. It's a dark, sad bar and sometimes people fight but nobody ever goes there looking to get laid. The snow is coming down and Anthony considers having a drink to unwind. Why does Brooke want to meet him? He moves toward a whiskey when Tommy pulls on his sleeve.

"I told you already," Anthony says raising his hand. "Don't you have somewhere to go?"

"Do I look like I have somewhere to go?" They face each other. "Buy me something to eat."

"You're not supposed to ask me for any more money."

"I'm not asking for money. They serve food in there." Tommy nods to the bar where one man has grabbed another by the collar of his shirt and a woman in a tiger-print dress leans her head back and lets out a laugh like a roar. "Buy me a double hamburger."

"I'll buy you a five-cent mint."

"What about just a hamburger."

"A pack of gum."

"A hot dog."

Anthony steps into the Lakewood and orders a hot dog and a whiskey on ice. "I'll cover that," the lady in the tiger-print shirt says.

"You better stay away from my woman," a small man next to Anthony says. "You can't afford it."

Anthony steps out of the bar and hands Tommy his hot dog.

"What about ketchup?"

Anthony goes back inside and takes a seat in front of his drink.

Morning time Brooke sits in the restaurant stirring cream and sugar into her third cup of coffee. She has been waiting for an hour but they never decided on a time to meet. For some reason Brooke thought that she and Anthony were synched onto the same schedule. As she stirs her coffee she knows she was wrong.

"Are you ready to order yet?" the waitress asks.

"I'm waiting for somebody," Brooke responds.

"You better leave a good tip," the waitress says. "You're taking up my section." Brooke doesn't know what the waitress means.

Anthony lowers himself into the booth across from Brooke. He wears blue jeans with holes in the knees that show the yellow long johns he wears underneath and a big blue jacket with a fake fur collar. The waitress lays down red plastic menus with pictures of farm animals next to the dishes. Happy chickens smile by the egg dishes. Happy pigs stand by the ham and bacon meals. Anthony scans the list quickly and then drops it back to the table. Brooke decides on pancakes and bacon and Anthony orders a cup of coffee.

Anthony doesn't like the restaurant. He doesn't like Saturday breakfast. The sound of chewing mixed with the smell of sausage. Even the trannies with their makeup wiped clean except for eyeshadow and their hair in rollers eat omelets and soup.

"The waitress hates me," Brooke says as the waitress puts Anthony's cup of coffee in front of him. He sips it black.

"Not everybody can like you."

The restaurant gets busier. People come in and sit wherever they want. The waitresses can't keep track of the people and the people come and go without paying their bills. Brooke chews on her pancakes. She eats three pancakes and then orders a glass of milk. She eats three pieces of bacon smothered in syrup. "I love this place," Brooke says. "I love to eat. That's probably why I'm so thin." She puts her fork down. "They took Lance. They took him off to jail." She drinks from her glass of milk. "They're holding him at the jail on 26th and California and they want one thousand dollars."

"Aren't you going to bail him out?"

"He doesn't have that kind of money. How could I bail him out?"

"You could use your money."

"Oh no. I couldn't do that." She pushes the empty plate toward the edge of the table.

"For throwing a couple of bottles," Anthony says. "He'll be back in no time."

"I'm not going to stay here," she tells him. "I'm going to go back home. I'm going to go back to Michigan."

"Better do it before it's too late."

"It's never too late. That's what my daddy told me. He said that it's never too late to start over and it's never too late to admit you made a mistake. I can go back anytime. I just want to wait a little while. I've enrolled in modeling school. Maybe you should enroll in modeling school too. They have a four-week program."

"To learn what? How to walk down a runway?" He takes a drink from his coffee, then he notices Brooke's big, sad eyes. "Don't look at me like that."

The waitress takes the plate. Brooke asks, "What do you do with your time?"

"I dance."

"You don't dance all the time."

"I exercise. I sit in my room. Sometimes I watch TV with the old man down the hall from me. I set my alarm to go off in the middle of the day and to go off at ten at night. Sometimes I read a book. And then I exercise."

"I work and I shop." Brooke says though she wasn't asked. "I like to do cocaine sometimes but Lance says it makes me talk too much but I don't think I talk too much. Do you think I talk too much?"

"Are you on cocaine now?"

"No."

"I don't think you talk too much."

"I know where we could get some cocaine if you want. There's a guy in our building that sells it. We could stop by and get some. If you want."

"I don't do drugs in the morning," Anthony tells her sipping his coffee. "It's not healthy."

"Oh. Well, what should we do?"

"How about nothing. What did you want to talk to me about?"

Brooke bites her lips and crosses and uncrosses her legs. She jerks across the table to touch Anthony's face. Anthony holds still as she runs her fingers along his cheeks. Anthony stares at her. His face is cruel and afraid but not violent. Brooke knows Anthony is an unhappy person but she doesn't know why. But they are in an industry. It would be a lie to say that everyone that strips, that turns tricks, that poses with their legs spread for some raunchy two-dollar magazine or five-dollar videocassette was damaged. It would be wrong to say that everyone in their industry, every hooker and hustler strutting their ass down Roscoe, was broken. But it would not be a lie to say most. Brooke knows Anthony is an unhappy person. She leans toward him, curious about his unhappiness. What could have happened? Where did he go wrong? She thinks she could help him because she is not an unhappy person like Anthony. She has goals, things she means to accomplish.

"Do you have a car?" Brooke asks. "I need someone to give me rides when I go on calls. Someone to hang out and wait for me. I could pay you eighty dollars. I think that's the going rate."

Anthony looks at Brooke as she pulls her fingers away. He looks at Brooke's cheeks, they're large enough to set a quarter on. He notices her leaning toward him. "Sure," he says. "I've got a car."

Lance walks the linoleum corridor to the housing blocks. He is assigned to a dorm three sleeping area. There are fifty beds single-tier in the low-ceilinged room, two steel toilets in the corner. Lance looks at the iron legs bolted to the floor and the spiderweb of steel over the windows. He looks for a weapon before settling on the faces. He smells industrial antiseptic. He hears wolf whistles under the glare of large white teeth.

In the corner four men play spades. One of them bids four, one of them calls yard. "That leaves one trick too many," one says.

"Guess somebody's got to lose," the other man says.

Some of the men are headed for division eleven, short-term maximum security. Some are off to Marion, some to Joliet, and others just couldn't make bail. This is a holding pen. Short time. Nothing much happens unless you're good -looking, small, and unlucky. Most of them are just docking their boats in another port in a prison nation. It doesn't take long for someone to approach Lance. It's the curse of every good-looking runaway.

"You look like someone who knows the rules," says a large man with thick braided hair. Lance turns away and the man pinches his shoulder. "What's your name?" The blue shirt in the office looks up from his newspaper and surveys the room then goes back to his reading, radio at his side.

The man playing cards says, "I'm tired of losing. Somebody else needs to lose for a change."

"Shit," says the other man. "I've been losing my whole life."

"No reason to stop now," says one and throws down the ace of spades.

"If you don't have a name I could give you one," says the man with the thick braided hair to Lance. "My name's John Jackal but you can call me JJ. I've been in this room for a month. Before that they had me in the SHU for stabbing this bitch with a sharpened toothbrush. But I've never hurt an OC, you know what I mean? I know my place." JJ speaks casually, all the time in the world. "Sheriff let me out of the hole. We made a deal. I've got friends on the outside. Do you understand what I'm telling you?" JJ pushes Lance's hair off his cheek with his large fingers.

A sharpened toothbrush, thinks Lance. It's a good idea.

While Lance is getting fucked in Cook County Jail, Anthony walks down to Happy Motors on Diversey and Clark. In his pocket he has his savings. It's worthless anyway. It's just money for a rainy day. He figures he can make the money back stripping in the clubs. As long as he can stay young enough.

The used car lot anchors the street and Anthony steps in the paths between the rusted hulks. He looks at the yellow Camaro, the black El Camino. On the corner a vendor with sunglasses sells elotes with butter and paprika for one dollar from a steaming white cart. The vendor's hands are stuffed deeply in his pockets and his neck swathed in a bright wool scarf. The car lot is on a six-corner intersection. Cars head toward the Loop down Milwaukee or to Clark Street down Division. Others speed away, to the suburbs, to Wisconsin. Chullos with nets in their hair and white smocks walk by on lunch break, suspicious. Behind all of the used and battered cars is a trailer and out of that trailer a tall Mexican wearing a cheap blue suit with a patch over his eye braves the cold to walk toward Anthony.

"Hello. My name is Cantor." Cantor sticks his hand out and Anthony takes it. "What kind of a car can I sell you."

"I have eight hundred in my pocket. Give me something that runs good. Something big."

"We don't have any cars that cost that little. That's not enough money to buy a car here. Don't you want a car?"

Anthony snorts.

"Perhaps we can get you some credit. Then you can have this nice El Camino over here. You could go anywhere. The banks would never catch you in a car this fast."

"I don't have any credit. I don't even have a bank account."

"Then how can I give you a car? What can I give you for eight hundred? There is nothing."

Anthony sweeps the snow-lined hoods with his gaze and then comes back to Cantor. "I guess I came to the wrong place." But as he is walking away Cantor grabs his sleeve.

"Here is the car for you."

They walk through the lot, between the bumpers, back toward the corner and Anthony wonders if Cantor has somebody back in the corner waiting to jump him and take his money. Cantor pulls Anthony along by his sleeve and Anthony's long blond hair blows back behind him. He turns and looks back at the man in the sunglasses selling elotes and the man smiles and waves an arm holding a pair of metal tongs. They stop and Cantor turns to Anthony quickly and Anthony sees a rusted-out 1975 Chevy Caprice, the car almost as big as Anthony's room. "This," Cantor says, "is your car."

"Yes," Anthony says. "This is the one."

Anthony easily steers the big car through the streets. The steering column seems to run into his forearm, responds to the weight of his biceps. He drives past the mural building with the paintings of all the Chicago athletes trying on shirts at Bigsby & Kruthers. He drives past Division, well past Lake Street. He drives past the Coca-Cola billboard and the I90-94 interchange.

He pulls the wheel and the car responds. Eight large cylinders of power rattle and hum beneath the long hood. The muffler shakes and pops and the carburetor pours gas down the engine's gullet. Long bench seats to fit a family of seven stretch from door to door. He passes smaller cars, pulls in the narrow spaces between them, dares them to hit him. The large car is an extension of Anthony and he drives it well.

Brooke sits besides him with the sun visor open staring at her face in the small mirror and patting it down with makeup. In a moment of insecurity she asks Anthony, "Do you think I'm pretty?" But it is just a moment. A young girl worried about her face.

Anthony doesn't answer Brooke until she finally says to get his attention, "I think you're pretty even if you don't think I'm pretty." He looks over at her. "That's what you want me to say, isn't it? Don't you like it when people tell you you're pretty? I think you do. And you know what? I do think you're pretty. I think you're pretty in the most unnatural of ways."

Anthony squints from her words. Sometimes Brooke speaking is like too much sunlight coming through a window.

They drive around the Loop. In Chicago the Loop is the series of interconnecting trains that circle the financial district. During the day the Loop is a parade of suits. Women in black skirts and black tops. Men in pinstripes, double-breasted. The Palmer House is the only hotel actually inside the Loop. Otherwise it is not zoned for residence. The Palmer House with its ridiculous doormen with large red feathers coming out of their hats is the exception to the rule. Chicago is founded on the exception to the rule.

Anthony drives Brooke smoothly along the highways of Chicago.

As they get more westward the trains join them. The blue line runs alongside the car, ducking below ground and then raising its steel-flecked head again to roar at the car.

Leaving the city they pass a giant water tank with a bright red rose painted on its side and then, coming back in, they land at O'Hare. "There," Brooke says, pointing to an exit. Anthony's fingers tighten on the wheel.

He pulls into the turnaround at the hotel and stops. Brooke steps out and disappears through the revolving door. Then he drives to the back of the lot and parks the car.

Anthony sits in the car for a minute and then gets out and goes into the hotel himself. While Brooke is gone up to room 1313 Anthony steps to the bar to order himself a drink. The bartender looks like a girl just past thirty. Her brown curly hair falls past her collar, she wears a ruffled white shirt and tight black pants with a maroon paisley vest. She gives Anthony her everyday smile and runs her fingers through her hair and smells the smoke that has nested there.

"What can I get you?"

"How about a port?"

"Lots of sugar in port. Make you fat." She leans over the bar. Her joke is lost on Anthony.

"What about whiskey?"

"Carcinogens. Give you a hangover. Won't be able to workout in the morning."

"What's best?"

"Always bet on red. Just kidding. All you can do is drink vodka and water and hope. No sugar. Low calories."

"That's what I'll have then."

"Vodka and water?"

"Yeah. That."

Anthony sips slowly on his drink, looking to kill the time. Brooke will give him eighty dollars. He figures he will only have to take her on ten runs to make the price of the car back. Except that the car eats lots of gas. He might have to go on fifteen runs to make it up. When he is done with his drink he pushes his glass forward and the girl fills it up. Four businessmen sit on the couches near the window talking. Their talk is foreign to Anthony. He focuses on the basketball game playing on the television in front of him. Orlando Woolridge pulls a windmill dunk out of thin air. The crowd goes wild. The Bulls are still losing by twenty points.

Orlando Woolridge has never once passed the ball.

Anthony drinks and fragments of conversation pass him. A group of analysts are in town for a trade show. Four of them sit at a table behind Anthony with a bowl full of spiced peanuts. They talk about business school. They talk about pharmaceutical stocks. They throw around words like "gross margin" and "branding exercise." He can't make sense of them. He can't make sense of their world. He doesn't want to make sense of their world. He doesn't want to contemplate the decisions people make and the reasons they make them. He doesn't want to worry about why people fall in love, why they need to get married, why junkies fall down the sidewalks chasing needles. He figures the answer is just the same anyway. They're all bored. Bored like he is. The businessmen chase money and stocks and then spend the money on fancy clothes that hide their bodies. Anthony thinks they spend the money on toupees. They spend it on Brooke, Anthony, and Lance. They are the ugliest people. They are bored and they chase the most worthless thing.

The girl asks Anthony how he feels and Anthony responds, "Like a pipe." She places a third drink in front of Anthony and he takes it worrying slightly about how he is going to get Brooke home safe and sound in his big orange car if he's drunk. He takes a sip and decides that if you drink alone then you have a problem. He worries about passing the time. He has not been on a stage in two days. His veins are itching for eyeballs and fingers.

"Smile about something," the girl says. "Or you'll make me regret being in the service industry."

Brooke taps Anthony's shoulder and he places his drink back on the bar. Brooke picks it up for him and finishes it in one gulp. "Vodka and water?" she says.

"It's good for you."
They get back in the Caprice and head for the city.

9.

THE JUDGE decides to let Lance out with a fine and the guards come to get him in heavy black boots. When the cop opens the gate JJ grabs Lance's hair. "Don't forget to come back and visit," he says. Then JJ lets go and Lance, rather than continuing through the gate toward the waiting cop, turns back to JJ who still smiles at him. Lance's mouth is cut and blood is crusted inside his nostrils.

"It's not that big of a world," Lance tells him. "And when I see you next I'm going to cut you into pieces and string your carcass from a tree."

JJ jumps from his bunk and Lance hits him squarely in the nose, breaking it. But it's not enough to stop him and he lands on top of Lance, punching him in his face. The other men in the cell holler and howl in approval. "You're mine, you hear me. You're mine. Always mine." The police come running in and pull the big man off Lance and beat him down with billy clubs and the other men step aside. Nobody wants a piece of the cops in their blue shirts.

The police scream nigger, coon, faggot. One of them grabs Lance roughly by the arm and squeezes. The rest of them whale on the big man and Lance can't even see the man under the pile of blue shirts and nightsticks. Lance lunges forward, "I'm going to kill you." The cop wraps a thick arm around Lance's throat and bangs him into the cell wall, he lifts Lance from the floor by his neck and squeezes the breath from his throat. More policemen come. Billy clubs swing madly through the room and the men hide in the corners. When Lance is yanked from the room he says to the pile of angry cops and the big man underneath them, "Sooner, rather than later." The cop drags him to checkout down the hall.

They give Lance back what was in his pockets except the money. He had stolen three hundred dollars from Brooke that day and he had made over a hundred from the Stolen Pony. They keep the money he stole from Brooke and give him all the crumpled singles. The cops laugh at Lance.

"Damn," they say. "At a dollar a blow job you must have been on your knees for a week." They all break up. "Ain't that about a bitch."

Lance smiles for them and sweeps all of his damaged money off the table quickly with one hand just like it was laying on the floor and walks out of the jail at 26th and California.

The jail is located in an area of Chicago known as the Wasteland. They call it the Wasteland because when Martin Luther King was shot the kids walked out of school and trashcans flew through the windows. Lightning broke the sky and fires raged above the West Side. Mayor Daley Sr. circled overhead in his helicopter wondering aloud, "Why are they doing this to me?" The residents pulled the cement from the walks. They tore the signs from the hotels, they scorched the earth. Their anger poured down the street like lava from an erupting volcano. This area burned down so all that is left are government buildings and vacant lots with brown grass and weeds in the summer and snow-covered dirt in the winter. That and the remaining buildings, all condemned and filled with homeless residents and heroin houses. Nobody wants to be stuck in the Wasteland. The Wasteland still smells of ash, and large white eyes watch from holes in the wood. Nobody is really sure where the Wasteland begins and where it ends, but they know it stretches from the West Side to the South Side of Chicago. Some places are definitely in the Wasteland. Garfield Park with its stately parkhouse and large, empty fountains is clearly in the Wasteland. Kilbourn and Washington with the row of burned-down houses is clearly in the Wasteland. When kids on the corners stand watch over abandoned cars with vacant yellow eyes and small machine guns tucked in their belts, they are clearly in the Wasteland. The rest is unclear. Washington Park is up for grabs. The University of Chicago is protected by the largest private police force in the country.

Lance feels the cracked buzz of the Wasteland while waiting for his bus in front of the jail. He looks back on the searchlight running along the jail blocks and the darkness ahead.

Lance rides the bus all the way north. Three days is too long to be in jail. He thinks back to his time spent as a child. He remembers getting up at six in the morning to do exercises and he remembers that every week a kid got knifed. When you knifed somebody you tattooed a teardrop under your eye to take responsibility and let the other kids know they shouldn't mess with you. He remembers his mother coming to see him on the weekends. She was there every Saturday and she would bring cookies. She cried harder every time another teardrop appeared on Lance's face. He didn't understand his mother's unhappiness. He had no answer to her questions. She would ask him, "What did I do wrong? What could I have done better for you?" He couldn't answer her questions because she had never done anything wrong to him. She always loved him no matter what. As a child she had given him anything he wanted. She would never bring her boyfriends home because she didn't want Lance to get the wrong impression. His mother with the long brown hair and her thin, drawn face and her wrinkled hands which she would wring as she spoke, his mother loved Lance beyond words. She loved Lance past imagination. When she looked she only saw Lance. But Lance was always bad. He got in fights. He threw tantrums. His mother loved her beautiful boy. Always the best-looking boy in every class, the wildest, most violent, most unpredictable. She stopped coming to the jail when Lance was seventeen. They told him she had an aneurysm and died suddenly. They told Lance his mother died painlessly. But the social workers whispered that she had died of regret.

Lance stretches out on the bus. He wants to get home to Brooke and go on a drug binge and forget the men that raped him in the jail. Sometimes beauty is a curse. He had been molested by several different teachers as a child in the juvenile hall. Every time he got locked up they attacked him. He fought them off but there were always too many. It got so that he didn't care that much, just gave it to them. But this time, the big man. He is going to remember the big man. Just for the hell of it.

He gets off the Belmont bus at Halsted. Walking into his building he is confronted with the usual stack of yellow pages and the silent doorman always standing at attention, never doing anything. He grabs the stack of yellow pages and pulls them to the floor. They fall in heaps and flopping piles. "What are you going to do about it?" he says to the doorman. The large books litter the entranceway spilling into the doorway and Lance lifts his legs high over them stepping to the elevator.

He rides the elevator and gets off a floor early to visit Rex. Rex lives in the apartment directly below Brooke and Lance. Rex hangs colored sheets from the windows to keep out the sun and has pizza delivered every two days. Rex sells Lance a rock and a pill and Lance goes up to his apartment and Brooke is not there.

Lance sees the clothes, the shades are down. Brooke and Lance also want to keep out the sun. He looks over the room staring into the hills of laundry looking for Brooke. She is not there but he keeps looking because he wants her to be there so badly that he tries to will it. He stands knee-deep in his own darkest fear, that Brooke will never return.

A broken tire pressure gauge sits over the fridge. He stuffs it with a rock and turns on the stove and then sucks the flame from the stove through the makeshift pipe and takes the fire and the smoke from the rock into his lungs and holds and holds and holds for as long as he can before coughing and falling to the ground holding his stomach. Almost immediately the euphoria takes over. The feeling of being able to do anything. Inside the fridge there is still a six-pack of beer and he cracks one open and the beer cools his burning mouth and then he punches the wall and his hand breaks.

Anthony pulls the big car in front of Brooke's building and she leans over to kiss him and he gives her his cheek. Brooke steps out of the car and Anthony steers the big car off toward home. She steps through the entrance and sees the doorman on his knees straightening out the stacks of yellow pages, some of which lie on the floor. "Takes time," he says to Brooke.

"I know," she replies and runs her hand through the

doorman's thick hair.

She rides the elevator up and swings open the door to the studio. Lance sits on a pile of clothes with a beer in his hand. The fire on the stove licks the air around it and illuminates an aluminum pipe with black markings around its horn.

"Oh," Brooke says to the room.

Lance takes a long drink and then rubs the can underneath his chin. He turns his head away from the can, his other hand gripping tightly to his knee. "Where have you been?" It's not a question, it's an accusation. "Where were you? You didn't come to visit me and you didn't wait for me to get home. Where were you? Don't you know? You do know. Don't you? What were you doing?" He takes another drink off the beer to stop his mania, to slow him down for a moment and Brooke knows she has walked into a trap. Brooke stands still and Lance twists his neck as far as it will go and opens and closes his mouth. He's trying to stretch his face. The rest of the room is motionless except for the fire sputtering on the stove.

"Maybe I should have some too," she says nodding toward the pipe, and that's when she notices Lance's swollen hand. "What did you do to yourself?"

"It's your fault. You did it to me. You were off fucking somebody. Spreading your legs for somebody. You were too busy fucking somebody else to care about me. That's what happened to my fucking hand."

"I do it for you, Lance. I do it because you want me to. I don't care about them."

Lance drops his beer on the floor and the beer pours out onto the clothes lying there. A puddle forms in the valley of two piles of cotton shirts and then soaks through. He jumps up and smacks Brooke in the mouth. He grabs her hair and throws her down and she lands face-down on her stomach. He pulls roughly at her skirt.

"Ow, Lance, you're hurting me."

"Shutup," he says. "Shutup. You always lie to me." He rips her panties off. "Is this how they fuck you? Like this? Do they all fuck you like this?"

Brooke buries her face in her hands. "Only you."

"That's right you fucking bitch. You fucking whore bitch." He pulls her hair and she pushes back into him but she is crying a little. He comes into her and she reaches out, grabbing yards of fabric, her fingers burrowing beneath purses and skirts. They all know, in the industry. It hurts, but it doesn't hurt as much as it would. She takes it and he pushes into her.

"Yes, Lance," she says. "Do it to me like that."

Anthony moves across the stage slowly. The still air of the afternoon offers little more than a tired bridge to the evening. Anthony looks from the five or six men nursing cheap beer at the bar to Henry's fat features. He tries to make out what song is being played. He has heard it before, but that was years ago.

The door opens as a man at the bar rubs his nose with his hand and says something to Henry. Lance steps through the bar, a trench coat draped over his shoulders, his damaged arm hanging in a cast from his neck. When Henry sees Lance a smile breaks across his mountainous face. Then the smile fades and Henry becomes worried and the men stop laughing and telling each other dirty jokes. Lance steals the air for a moment. He climbs the stairs and the men let out a collective gasp. Lance meets Anthony on stage and somebody spills a beer. The lights are low and while the Stolen Pony always smells of men and ruined beer, today it smells even more so. Anthony grinds against the lights, touching himself gently, looking up at Lance mockingly, and sliding his naked back over the squares with his feet tucked up behind his knees. Lance walks over him, stamping his foot near Anthony's shoulder. Lance walks around Anthony on the small square. He drops his coat to the floor. The men holler. The men throw dollar bills and fives and tens onto the lighted square.

Henry yells to his gaggle of lonely men, mouths open and wet with spit. "Welcome to my dark country, gentlemen. Welcome to my fields, my farm, my arena. Welcome to a land unlike any you have been to before or will go to again. Welcome to the end. Leave your loneliness at the door."

Anthony, standing now, is already down to a thong and the lights play through the rips in his chest, his well-defined stomach, the thick muscles in his legs. Lance takes his shirt off and throws it to someone sitting at the bar. "I know about your car," he hisses in Anthony's ear. "I know about it."

Anthony swings around, bumps his chest against Lance's chest, wraps an arm over Lance's shoulder, presses his leg into Lance's leg. "Hit a woman hard enough," he says, "and I suppose she'll tell you anything."

Lance pushes away, kicks off his boots, unbuckles his jeans. "I'll kill you," he says and nobody hears him say it because the music is too loud, nobody except Anthony whose ear is close to Lance's mouth. "I will."

Anthony smiles. Lance's breath bounces off his ear. He feels the stares from the bar. Anthony looks at Lance. He knows Lance is crazy and he knows Lance will live effort-lessly and for a short time. "Save your anger," he tells Lance.

"Your anger is wasted on me."

They circle one another. Anthony dancing, Lance just strutting. Anthony knows how to dance because the music controls him and Lance knows how to get the dollar bills because he doesn't care, he doesn't hate the men at the bar the way Anthony does. And now Anthony dances around behind Lance, sweeping Lance, and wraps his strong arms across Lance's chest and pulls him close, his nose in Lance's hair. Anthony rests his head in the crook of Lance's neck and smells his collarbone. Lance stands in front of Anthony with Anthony's head on his shoulder. While Anthony dances Lance stands in front and works the crowd.

10

IT'S MORNING time. A thick, slushy snow falls from the sky and fills in the grooves of the tire rims and banks the concrete of the curbs, the snow buries Chicago alive. Lance and Brooke stand in the snow in front of the boarding home. Lance demands the keys to Anthony's car and pushes eighty dollars toward him. Anthony snatches the money and throws the keys at Lance who drops them and then has to dig through the snow to pick them up. Brooke stares at Anthony, her lips parted, and Lance tucks the keys in his pocket and waits.

Lance does not drive as well as Anthony in the same way he cannot dance as well as Anthony. If Lance and Anthony were joined together they could perhaps be one perfectly miserable person, but instead they are separate and miserable, and neither of them is perfect.

Brooke sits next to Lance as they drive along the streets. Thick slush pelts the windshield. Lance finds himself immersed in insecurity staring at Brooke who only looks ahead through the windshield wipers. Lance gave Anthony the eighty dollars Brooke would have paid for the ride. Brooke had protested on the way to the boarding house. "No, it's silly," she said but Lance didn't hear her. Brooke didn't think Anthony was going to give Lance the keys to his car but he did.

Lance slides through the snow. Brooke thinks of Anthony throwing the keys at Lance, like he didn't care at all. Lance looks from the snowy road to Brooke's face and back to the road. Lance is almost lucid for a moment as the questions work their way through his deranged mind. Finally, one bubble of thought rises to the surface, one single voice speaks on top of all the noise:

"I love her, but she doesn't love me."

He looks at Brooke with a renewed longing. Her black eye is evident beneath the makeup. He wants to drink her. He wants to have her in a cup. He wants to inhale her. He wants every part of Brooke's young body, her long legs, her thin arms, schoolgirl face. He wants her completely. He desires her so strongly that even having her could never be enough.

He touches her arm and as he does so she looks at her watch. His other arm in a sling, he pulls his hand quickly back to the wheel and they barrel over a bridge into the land of Lincoln Avenue motels.

Lincoln Avenue is packed with cheap motels and neon-lit Mexican restaurants. All of it a slush-filled haze in the morning. They pass the Starz Motel, the Apache, the Clean and Simple, fifty a week or fifteen a night. A bunch of run-down motels and rooms without phones. Someone tried to build a shopping mall once across the street and now it's just a series of empty white buildings on a gravel lot. Each motel room has a large bed and a larger TV and a door. Truckers stay in the rooms. Alcoholics stay in the rooms and fill up on seventy-five-cent Budweisers down at Myrtl's. The drug addicts stay there. The motel owners don't want to know. There is only one rule in the land of Lincoln Avenue motels, No Credit. Pay or leave.

Lance and Brooke pull into the parking lot and Brooke says, "Wait here." Lance has never been good at communicating. His mouth hangs open but no sound comes out. In his stomach he wants to apologize for her swollen eye. He wants to promise not to steal from her, not to hit her. A strange rattle emanates from his throat as he watches Brooke's legs step easily from the passenger seat clad in her trademark black stockings. The rattle startles Brooke and she turns to Lance whose mouth hangs open. Brooke kisses him on the cheek with one leg out in the snow, the way a mother kisses a child who is about to throw a tantrum. And then she is gone.

Lance bites at his fingers for a moment. He hates the snow piling up on the hood of Anthony's car. In fact, he hates the car. The car is too large, too loud, too ugly and smells of gasoline. He thinks about driving the big car at high speed into a brick wall with Brooke and himself inside.

The motel is called the Valentine Inn. Lance unlatches the door and stands outside the car in the wet snow. Over him the yellow sign flashes on and off, its unwanted message: "Welcome." He thinks Brooke went into room number 108. The snow makes it hard to see. Every time he starts to think his mind goes to Brooke's shoes, Brooke's ears, Brooke's nose, Brooke's mouth. Brooke's mouth swallows Lance's spinning mind. Brooke's mouth whispers something to Lance while they sleep. The noise in Lance's head is deafening.

Lance stands in front of room 108 contemplating the motel door and then walks across the street to the liquor store. The store, lit in white neon, sells two kinds of beer, one kind of whiskey, one kind of vodka and a variety of cheap wines. An old man behind the counter chews on a toothpick and reads the newspaper. When Lance walks in the man doesn't look up, he just hears the bells. Lance pays for a pint of whiskey and the man takes the money and gives the change on instinct. Then he turns the page.

Lance sits in the car and drinks. The alcohol quiets the noise in his head. When he met Brooke he was doing construction up in Grand Falls, Michigan, and she was a fifteen-year-old girl returning home from school. Lance followed on the scent of her perfume. He walked her home listening the whole time to her talk about her favorite bands and what clothes she liked to wear. One thing about Brooke, she sure could talk. When they got near her house, a mansion with a thick iron gate, she told him he had to leave. She didn't want her daddy getting jealous. Lance persisted. Every day he walked her home. The other girls whispered about Brooke's boyfriend with the tattoos on his face. The other girls were jealous because Brooke had the most rock 'n' roll boyfriend of them all.

One day Lance interrupted her during another long monologue about her new favorite band. He said, "Let's go to Chicago." And she said, "OK. Just for a while." And that was it.

Forty-five minutes have passed with Lance drinking in the car. Lance steps out of the car and throws the bottle into the snow. Then he steps on the bottle with the heel of his boot. Lance bangs on the door to the room. It feels like the snow and the cold is getting inside the cast on his arm and squeezing his fractured hand. When no one answers he bangs on the door harder, and when the door does open Lance is staring into the barrel of a shotgun.

The man's face resembles tree bark. His hands are steady, his gun is steady. He sizes up Lance and decides he doesn't like Lance's long hair. "What are you looking for, boy?"

"I'm looking for my girl."

"That your woman over there?" He nods to Brooke lying on the bed with her top off, her small naked breasts poking forward, her legs bent, her panties still on, garter belt, shoes and skirt and top lying on the side of the bed next to a cheap dresser.

"Yes."

"What you date a prostitute for?" The man cocks the gun. The click rumbles through Lance's ears but all he hears is Brooke saying she loves him. Brooke looks around the room. She doesn't know what to do. She is chewing gum. "Why you want to do that and then come barging in on me when I'm trying to have a good time?" The man smacks the barrel into Lance's forehead and Lance falls back against the wall and slides down to the floor. A raised red welt appears quickly on Lance's forehead. "You know your little girl sucked my dick. You know she told me it's the best dick she's ever seen. What's wrong with you that makes her say that?" The man lands his heavy boot in Lance's side and puts the gun down. Lance looks up from the floor at the man. He has made a mistake. Brooke could never love this man. Lance's nostrils fill with the smell of boot leather.

Brooke sits up in the bed pulling her top over her tiny breasts. "Leave him alone," she says.

"You talking to me or him?" the man asks.

She feels scared and tired of violence. The man opens the door and allows the wintry air into the room with its depressing image of a snow-filled parking lot. He buries his boot one more time in Lance's side and Lance throws up blood and drink. The man steps past Lance and out of the room. He leaves the door open and the snow from outside falls on Lance. The man opens the door to a shit-brown Thunderbird and throws his gun inside. "You two kids have fun tonight." The engine turns over and the man drives away. Lance catches the license plate, it reads Minnesota.

Brooke holds a cold rag up against Lance's head. He has become helpless. She strokes his cheek. Half of her is so angry that he would come in like that, jealous of a trick, and the other half has moved away. "It doesn't make any sense, Lance. Why would you do that? What did you think you would see?" He looks to her and she looks to him. It is over and they both know it. They leave the room for the bar down the street. They sit on the red velvet stools and someone plays sad country music on the jukebox. They drink away the day in the bar, sad and wounded, until the night comes.

11

BROOKE STANDS naked in her room surrounded by piles of clothes and the sound of breath. She deliberately pulls the blinds up and the sun streams through the windows of the apartment, coating her pale skin. She places her hands against the cold window pane. The blinds have never been up in the morning. The sun pours across her naked legs and the black tuft of hair between them. The sun streams over the clothes on the floor. It forms pools in the valleys between the hills of laundry. Brooke wants to swim in the sunlight that forms the pools. Brooke's clothes cover every available space. The piles are full of tiny white tops, little black skirts. Tights linger in balls. Lingerie, boots, gold-trimmed panties, leather bras, strap-on dildos, whips, fuzzy handcuffs. She surveys all of the clothes she has bought in the last two years while they have been living in this place. She has purchased new clothes almost every day. She has never once done her laundry, it never occurred to her.

The sunlight falls gently across Lance's sleeping head and she sees the welts from the gun where the man hit Lance last night. The welts form an infinity sign. Lance sleeps in the same jeans he wore in the snow with a thick black belt around the waist. She hears Lance breathing and it's clear why she has loved him. His lips twitch under the stream of light. He represents what so many women want, a man to protect her, a boy to take care of.

Brooke starts to pull apart the fruits of her labor, piles of dirty clothes. She looks for things she can take with her because she is going to leave. She pulls apart pile after pile rearranging and creating more piles of dirty clothes. She doesn't find anything. Thousands and thousands of dollars worth of hotel rooms, blow jobs, latex and condoms, and not a thing worth taking along. She has spent two years building nothing. From a green Marshall Field's bag in the corner she pulls out new nylons, a new skirt. She starts to dress and Lance stirs. His eyes open to the sight of pantyhose running up Brooke's long, thin legs and the sunlight shining off the hose and the sun in his eyes making him squint.

"Don't go," he whispers from the mattress. "Don't go, Brooke. Don't leave me like this."

"I have to."

He pushes himself up and looks out of the window. He stands at the window frowning. He hates that the window is open, raining the sun on his home. He hates the sun and the outdoors. He hates the smell of fresh air, especially rolling off the lake in the morning. He thirsts for darkness and confinement. He hates the outside. From the window he can see the tops of other buildings covered in a layer of snow, the alley below thick with white fur. Brooke waits for him. He turns to her. He grabs Brooke. She is only half dressed and he pulls her into him with his one good arm and feels her small nipples against his chest. She doesn't try to resist him but stays against him with her arms at her side.

"I don't want you to go. Why are you going? Why did you stop loving me?" His face is so close to hers that he could bite her nose.

"I don't know."

"So it's true. Like I said. You don't love me."

"It is true. I don't love you anymore."

He pushes her away and she slams into the wall. She falls to the floor. He opens his palms. "Oh God. I'm sorry, baby. I didn't mean that."

"You meant it when you did it," she says. "But you don't mean it now."

"What are you saying? Why are you talking that way?" He pulls his long hair and then goes to the fridge and sees that there are only two beers. He knows Brooke won't want one in the morning. He opens one and takes a good long drink. "Why the hell wouldn't you love me? I haven't changed. I've never once changed. How the fuck can you decide to just stop loving me? How can you stop loving me when I haven't changed?"

"I never said I was going to stay with you. I just said I would go to Chicago to pass some time but now time has passed. It's just like I said. Don't act like it's a big deal. You always make a big deal out of everything."

"You never loved me. You just said you loved me. You can't stop loving someone unless you never loved them at all."

Brooke doesn't respond. There is no point in disagreeing with Lance. She did love Lance. She believes a person can fall in and out of love. When she looks at him now she has no desire for him. The urge to hold him has gone. She knows that she loved him because she used to want to hold him all the time. There is no point in disagreeing. She doesn't want to hurt Lance. She doesn't hate him. Hate is too close to love.

Lance looks at Brooke sitting half-naked on the floor. I should kill her, he thinks. Better dead than my enemy. But he pushes the thoughts out of his head and as soon as he does he wants her again. He wants to fuck her right now, on the floor. He can smell her body, her smell steaming off the tops of the piles of clothes. He puts the beer down and moves over to her unbuckling his pants. Brooke watches him coming, stumbling, peeling his pants off. The apartment is not large enough to accommodate Lance's lust, nor strong enough to turn him down. His lust is like a barely controlled rage bound only by the limitations of his own skin. Brooke lays back, lifting her skirt. He kneels in front of her between her legs and runs his hands on the back of her thighs. His fingers shake while his plaster cast moves along her skin. He leans forward and plants a kiss on her cheek. He smells her face and she turns her gaze toward the floor. He opens his mouth and lightly bites her cheek before ripping a large hole in her hose. He goes down between her legs, burying his chin, tasting and smelling her. He wants to get all the way inside. He rubs his face against her, his cheek, his eyelids, his chin, he wants to roll in her smell. He wants to be coated in her scent. He wants her to want it. He wants her to want him. He wills it and she doesn't respond. She lies in front of him and squirms but she doesn't say anything. He looks for her eyes but she is looking away. Finally he just enters her and she takes it from him without any resistance or pleasure. Just like she is waiting for a movie to end. Lance pushes into her harder and harder with violence. He squeezes her shoulder. He wants to get all the way inside. He tries to grab her with his broken hand but slips and hits the floor. The sweat pours down his face. He wants to rip her in two. He wants to kill her. He pushes so hard he is screaming. Finally he comes inside her. Covered in sweat, he wipes himself off with a shirt sitting on top of a pile.

"That's the last time I'll ever fuck you bitch. You fucking whore. I'm not a trick. I'm not your fucking trick." He stands up and stares down at her still lying on the floor. She covers her face with her arm then he spits on her naked stomach and he grabs his beer from the counter. He kills it in one swallow and then hurls the empty can against the wall. She wipes the spit off and resumes getting dressed.

They don't talk more to each other. Lance stands by the counter, his lips falling toward his chin. Brooke fully dressed puts on a pair of dark black shades. Lance finishes his last beer. "Hey, give me some money before you go. I need to buy some more beer."

"Oh, I couldn't do that, Lance. I couldn't leave you my money. I might not see you again for a long time. When would I get it back?" They stand across from each other and Lance can't tell what she is thinking because of her sunglasses. In one quick movement she is out. She closes the door behind her and Lance heaves the beer can at the door and it hits the door and falls to the floor. Glasses and plates follow. He looks at the clothes, all the leather, expensive lingerie. He lights the stove deciding to burn all of it to the ground and then changes his mind. He will take it in bags down to the vintage store on Halsted. On Halsted it is always fashionable to wear a whore's pants. Men walk around on Halsted in little girl's tight leather pants trying to sell their asses to the passing cars. The men on Halsted buy the clothes that belonged to all the runaway girls. The vintage stores specialize in runaway fashions. He will take what is left of Brooke, that bitch, in bags down to the vintage stores on Halsted and sell her off and then he will get drunk. But maybe he'll keep just a few items, to remember her, because he loves her so much. He loves her so much that it feels like his bones are turning to dust.

Brooke walks the staircase of the boarding house keeping her fingers loosely on the dark wooden banister. The banister shakes. A man falls past her, his fingers brushing her skirt with the scent of liquor. The man stops at the bottom of the stairs to watch Brooke walk away. As she gets to the top it becomes darker. The hallway light is out and two wires hang from the socket. The hallway is dark with just slits of light coming from under doors. A little light comes up the stairs from the window in the entranceway. She stands on the dirty red carpet and knocks on the door to Anthony's room and waits for an answer. There isn't one. She clutches her purse and stares down the hallway. The hallway is composed of small sounds. She hears a toilet flush. A door opens and closes. She hears an old man's scratchy voice say, "Fuck you, you don't know anything." After half a minute she yells, "Anthony, are you there?"

"I'm here," she hears from the room down the hall. She follows the yellow velvet. Anthony is sitting in a chair wearing blue jeans and a grey sweathood without shoes across from Mr. Gatskill and they are watching television. Anthony looks up and nods to her. She stays at the edge of the room in the doorway.

"Come in come in," Mr. Gatskill says to Brooke. "Good lord girl if you aren't damn fine looking. Like some whiskey? I've got whiskey. It's a special occasion."

"What's so special about it?"

"Anthony's never had a visitor from the outside. Nobody's ever looked for him before. This is the first time he has been searched out. That's special." Anthony scowls at Mr. Gatskill and Mr. Gatskill chuckles to himself and slaps his knee. Brooke likes the drunk old man sitting there in his pajamas watching a silent television set. "So you gonna have a cocktail girl or what?"

"Sure," Brooke says. "As long as everyone is having a

party." She sits down on the floor near the silent television pushing her skirt up under her. The screen is scratchy and the console full of dust. Anthony notices how much clearer the girl is than the television screen but doesn't know which he prefers.

"Got a love tap there," Anthony says motioning toward Brooke's eye.

"Here's your cocktail." Mr. Gatskill leans forward and hands her the bottle and she takes a sip. It's not really what she had in mind. The sour whiskey burns down her throat. She hands the bottle over to Anthony but he refuses. "Have a drink you bastard!" Mr. Gatskill yells.

"You know I don't drink before the evening."

Brooke feels silly now just drinking with the old man and hurriedly pushes the bottle back to him. The three of them don't say anything. Anthony just sits in his chair and Mr. Gatskill sips on his bottle. Then Brooke says, "I'm going home."

"How you getting there? You walking?"

"No. I'm going to go to the bus station and take a bus. I'm going back to Grand Falls, Michigan." Anthony thinks about the money he sank into the car and how he won't be able to get it back now. Maybe he can find other young hookers to drive around but he can't imagine where he would meet them. Maybe Brooke has friends. Maybe he can sell the car. Maybe he could deliver pizza.

"That's stupid," Anthony says.

"What's stupid?" Mr. Gatskill chimes in. "You calling each other stupid already? Jesus fuck. I was married twenty years before I started calling my wife stupid. You gotta hold your tongue boy. How you gonna make any friends?"

Brooke laughs and Anthony tries to focus on the television. He wonders why he ever comes over here except that he doesn't have his own television. He wonders why he watches television. All the dumb shows about dumb people doing nothing. Orphans living out in some farm community. Black suburban families, New York photographers. Anthony hates television but he watches television in Mr. Gatskill's room anyway.

"I spent the better part of my life married to that woman," Mr. Gatskill starts and Anthony moves to get up but sees that Brooke is interested. "I spent many years with her. We had what you would call a tempestuous relationship. When I met her I was just a kid in my twenties, like you two."

"I'm seventeen," Brooke says.

"I'm thirty-four."

"I don't give a fuck how old you are dammit. Where's my bottle?"

"In your hand."

Mr. Gatskill takes another drink. "I loved that woman. She was in medical school when I met her and both of her parents were doctors. 'Course, wasn't common for a girl to be a doctor back in those days. I was kind of a bum myself, a drifter. What you might call a 'Make Do Man.' At the time I met her I was bartending and she was checking out the other side of the tracks. Her parents hated me. First time I met her father he whispered he would gut me soon as the opportunity presented itself. Still, we did OK. I became a manager. She made much more money than me, you bet your ass. But I didn't care about money much one way or the other. Still don't. Problem was there was another man. A friend of mine. Tall fella with thick black hair. He worked down by the rail yard. We had been in school together as kids. We all used to play cards together, me, Mickey, a few of the other guys, my wife. Mickey and my wife, they had a kind of special relationship. S'pose I could have divorced her but I couldn't imagine living without her. We kept on going, not talking about it much. She would sneak off and I would pretend not to notice." Mr. Gatskill takes a large breath and a large drink of whiskey. "Finally we talked about it. I said to her, why have you been cheating on me all these years? What did I do to you? She said it was because I was a coward and if I had had the guts to tell her I loved her and that I didn't want to share her with anyone else then all of this wouldn't have happened." He waves his fingers around the room like there is fabric in his hands. "So it was my fault for not having the guts to tell her I loved her. Oh, well. You pay the price for playing it cool. It's too bad you only get to go through it once."

"Would you have divorced her quicker if you could do it again?" Brooke asks. "Would you have never fallen in love with her?"

"No. Nothing like that. Nothing like that. Nothing like that at all. I would have taken her somewhere far away from anyone and I would have told her I loved her every day." His eyes turn to glass and Anthony knows the story is over for now but he knows the other parts as well. He knows all of it. He's watched the silent television with the old man babbling often enough to pick up all the fragments of Mr. Gatskill's tragic past.

"What was her name?" Brooke asks.

"Mindy, Mindy..." The old man stares ahead chewing on his lower lip. He waves his fingers around the space in the room and gestures to someone who isn't there. Anthony stands up and grabs Brooke and pulls her out of the old man's room.

"But I want to hear more," Brooke says.

"Well you won't hear any more today. He's got nothing left to say right now and it all amounts to the same thing anyway. Don't fall in love, ever, because love is bad." Anthony opens the door to his room and Brooke follows him in. The room has one window facing a red brick wall. She sees the enormous mirror in the corner across from the mattress.

"Gee, it's a small room to have such a large mirror." They hear a buzzing and Brooke digs in her purse. "Oh, it's a call."

Anthony looks away disinterested. "Are you going to go? Are you going to answer that call? Why don't you go and do whatever it is you want."

Brooke thinks about it. She thinks about the man in the hotel room last night and the things that man said to Lance. Those weren't nice things and Lance was already feeling so bad after being in jail for three days. She thinks about that man and the lies that man told.

"I don't have to," she says. "I have enough money and my father will give me more money when I get home. He buys me anything I want. I've never really needed to work. Really, the only reason I have been working these last two years is because I was always told it was important to make your own money. You can't rely on other people for handouts. You don't rely on other people for handouts do you?"

"No. I don't."

"That's good. Because you're not supposed to." She looks back into her purse. "And even if you don't need money you should still work. Work is good for you."

"Your dad told you those things?"

She nods.

The thin light from the window backlights Anthony

standing with his hands in his pockets. Brooke bites a little on the inside of her mouth. There are things you can never learn when you are rich and beautiful and Brooke always has been. There are things you can never learn when you are poor and ugly because there are too many meetings where you are not invited. When Anthony was in the hospital as a child locked up for his own protection and then afterwards when he was placed with a large, religious family, he was always poor and he was always ugly. So the two of them look at each other but they look at each other differently. Brooke looks at Anthony from the view that things always work out for the best and Anthony notices Brooke's pretty young face from the perspective that things are not OK and they never will be. The huge mirror in the corner reflects both of them and their positions but it also sees the proximity of their fingers.

"I'm going to tell you something," Anthony says to Brooke. "You're just a kid. And you shouldn't listen to everything your father tells you or anyone else for that matter."

Brooke chews on her lip some more, deciding what to do. There are buses leaving for Michigan every hour. There is no hurry. She thinks Anthony is so pretty in his old blue jeans and hooded sweatshirt halfway unzipped and showing his naked chest. She notices a necklace hanging there. There is no hurry. She sits on the old bed and Anthony stands by the window. She smoothes out the spot next to her but Anthony doesn't respond.

"You could come with me to Michigan. My dad could get you a job. He's good at getting people jobs." Brooke's pager buzzes again and she turns it off. Then she smiles. "He says there is always work for people that are willing to work hard. You could come with me. We could drive there."

She sits on the bed with her legs crossed high and

Anthony wonders if she is inviting him. He thinks she is young and unsure of her own actions.

"Go to Grand Falls, Michigan? Leave Chicago? No way. I'm not going to Michigan and I don't work hard. I only do what I have to. Sometimes less."

"I don't believe that. You work hard. You exercise all the time. You don't naturally look that way."

"What way?"

"The lines in your face. You weren't born with those. I could tell when I saw you and Lance dancing and then when I saw you at Berlin. You work hard. You don't think so but you do."

Anthony makes a small move toward the bed. "Well, whatever. I'm not interested in working for your father and I'm sure not going to Michigan." He looks away. "Michigan," he says like a cough, almost laughing. He shakes his head.

Now there is nothing left to say but Brooke does not want to leave. She wonders if she leaned back in the bed if she could seduce Anthony but she realizes quickly that it wouldn't work. She is not ready to get on that bus, that long bus ride back to Michigan.

"Why won't you come to bed with me?" she asks.

"Forget it," he tells her. "Stop talking so much non-sense." He looks about his own room like it is a strange place.

"Just come and lie down. You should take a break."

He stares at her long legs and little skirt. He goes over to his closet and pulls out a pair of grey sweatpants and a big white T-shirt. "Put these on," he tells her and drops them on the bed next to her. He stands over her for a second and then steps out into the hall and pulls the door closed behind him. In the hall he can hear the sound of someone crying coming from a room in the darkness. The hallway is often lit with the sound of someone crying. He pushes it out of his head because he doesn't want to think about it.

Anthony waits a couple of minutes and then goes back into his room. Brooke's black tights and skirt and little top lie on the floor. Anthony's room is very clean and the small pile of clothes stands out. Brooke lies on his bed in his sweatpants and T-shirt, both of which are far too large for her small frame. She looks different without all of the tight black clothing. She looks like a child, more innocent. She lies straight with her long legs fully stretched. Anthony climbs into bed next to her. He reaches down and pulls the blanket over them and the two of them drift off into a comfortable, much-needed sleep.

Another sunny day but the wind is biting and cold. Anthony jogs west along Irving Park and turns on Damen. He passes the tattoo parlor there where Guy Atchinson works. Guy is one of the most famous people in the Chicago Underground. People come from all over the world for his body art. Famous musicians line up outside his door with their guitars on their shoulders. The store is closed and Anthony continues past into Polish town.

Brooke left this morning. She walked out of Anthony's room wearing his sweatpants and top with her little jacket. She left her tights and her skirt on the floor. She looked younger than ever in the oversized sweatsuit and heels. She stood by the door and said to Anthony who lay on the bed with his arms behind his head staring up at her, "Well, here I go." She tossed her arms in the air. She smiled broadly, pushing her large cheeks up over her eyes.

"Well, there you go," Anthony responded and Brooke's cheeks dropped just for a second before she left. Anthony looked across the room to the large reflection of himself staring back from the mirror. "Dammit," he said. The reflection of himself did not move. "Dammit," he said again. Then he got dressed and started running.

A dentist has hung a large sculpture of a toothbrush over the entrance. The Davis movie theater is playing a re-release of the *Star Wars* trilogy. Anthony runs along the streets trying to remember the night and put together what transpired. What did Brooke whisper last night? She whispered to the mirror while Anthony was sleeping behind her holding his arm against her stomach. "You are a sad and lonely person," she said and Anthony heard her in his sleep and was tormented in his dreams.

Anthony dreamt that he was above the world in heaven and God was there with a long flowing white beard. God wore a silver robe and Anthony's parents were seated uncomfortably on wooden stools. His foster parents were there as well and they kept their heads down and had Bibles open in front of them. His foster parents were praying but they weren't praying for Anthony's soul, they were praying for their own. Anthony wondered why they were praying for themselves and not for him when he so clearly needed their prayers more than they did. He thought they were selfish. The room they were in was made of marble, and paintings hung from the walls without any nails or tape. Brooke sat with Satan on a flaming chair further away. She sat on Satan's large red leg, her legs spread over his one leg. She was leaning back into him and moaning. Sweat poured down her face and her thin cotton shirt was stuck to her skin. Her legs were spread and her skirt rode up. Satan's large hand played absently between her legs and she squirmed from the heat. Against one wall was a small stage and Lance strutted back and forth spreading his arms out and beckoning to an absent crowd with all of his fingers, lewdly sticking his tongue out of his mouth.

Anthony thought he was on trial and he stared at his jury. A police officer ran through the room smashing at the walls with his baton stick then disappearing. Colored lights went on and the room was engulfed in pastel colors flashing off the Bibles and his parents' passive faces. A sea of people rose from beyond the room, their arms stretching out, their bodies moving in gigantic waves. Then Anthony realized he was not on trial but they were. It was he who was accusing them. He looked at Brooke and Lance and his parents and he jumped from his seat. "I blame you," he said to God and then ran across the room and jumped into the arms of the world, of all of the people in all of the world and the arms grabbed at his body and tore him to pieces.

Anthony runs past the Green Mill in Uptown. The Green Mill was Al Capone's bar and inside there are plush velvet seats and huge paintings but it is no longer a gangster hangout like it was during the Prohibition. Now there is jazz six nights a week and on Sundays they have a poetry slam and people come from all over the city and from the suburbs and walk down the dangerous streets to the old bar to read their poems and spill their fears for a crowd full of poets who can't wait to do the same. Anthony passes the Aragon Ballroom.

By the time Anthony is back at home he has run five miles. He does his push-ups, sit-ups, chin-ups. It is not enough. He looks at himself in the mirror. His face is covered in sweat and his cheeks are flushed red. He does not remember enough of his dream, just that he didn't sleep well, he never does.

12

BROOKE CATCHES the number eight Halsted bus. The bus passes all the bars. The snow is coming down heavily and Brooke sees Halsted Street through a white blanket. The bus passes along the edge of Downtown where Brooke gets off. The televisions in the store windows across from the Greyhound station say it is going to be one of the coldest Christmas Days on record, but they say that every year.

Brooke's Greyhound sloughs through the thick snow in the small towns between Chicago and Detroit. The towns on the eastern end of Chicago are both ugly and beautiful. They are industrial art projects belching thick reams of pollution onto the edge of Lake Michigan. Enormous nitrous candles fire the sky along the highway in the refuse of truck cabs and mini-cranes. Brooke passes through Hegwich. Brooke passes through Gary, Indiana, home of the Jackson family. Brooke sits in the middle of the bus. Behind her the convicts smoke cigarettes and in front of her mothers quiet their children. She notices the paper bags being passed across the aisle. As day becomes night Brooke fixes on the driver's reflection in the rearview mirror, a dark-skinned man with black stubble on his chin. He wears his sunglasses even as the sun goes down and the sky becomes black.

Four hours down the road the Dixie truckstop shines like a glowing yellow beacon toward the highway. The parking lot is littered with eighteen-wheelers. "You've got twenty minutes," the driver announces. "The poker machine pays in full at the candy counter, the bathrooms are on the left side of the building. If you're not back we'll leave without you. It wouldn't be the first time."

Brooke walks the pasted, fluorescent hallways past small counters selling homemade fudge. There are video games, gambling machines, gift shops, truck parts, and restaurants. She walks through the halls and finds a general store where she buys a pair of day-glo orange gym shoes and throws her heels in the trash. In her gym shoes and sweatpants and thick winter jacket the truckers don't look at her. She walks through the truck stop as a little girl whose father is close by. No one pays her any attention because she is just a skinny little girl and only sickos and perverts prey on little girls in sweatpants and gym shoes. The rest pay hookers to come to their hotel rooms in black lingerie, a running motor parked out front. Little girls have to watch out for sickos. Prostitutes have to watch out for everybody else. But the sickos don't come to Brooke because she is beyond them, she knows too much, and the truckers don't pay any attention to her because she is just a little girl. She feels what it feels like to be anonymous in a crowd.

"I fell in love once real bad," the waitress in the cafe says to Brooke. Her dirty blonde hair falling unevenly past her shoulders she goes from stool to stool refilling coffee. "I got hurt and dropped here by one of these trucker slimeballs." She hitches a thumb in the direction of everyone. "They're all the same." Brooke thinks the waitress sounds like a song. Brooke buys a candy bar, a magazine, and a bag of potato chips and gets back on the bus.

Before Detroit the bus stops in Ann Arbor. Brooke's father went to school here. His certificate from the University of Michigan Law School hangs proudly in his office. He always told Brooke that a good education is very important if you are going to provide for yourself in this world and if you are going to make a difference. She strains to see the school through the bus windows but the bus doesn't pass by the university. All she gets to see are strip malls and split-level-housing apartment complexes. A little ways off she can see the two square white pillars of University Hospital. She should have attended her modeling school classes but she was so tired that first morning that she didn't get up. Instead she lay in bed with Lance. They didn't say anything that morning but she could feel Lance's arms. He held her, his hand over her belly. She could feel Lance not wanting her to go. Lance never wanted her to go. Lance wanted to own her and here she is. Lance loved her deeply and she knows it. She knows what it is to be loved deeply by someone who cannot love anyone and how it feels to be needed by someone who can't be helped. She is in Michigan now, rapidly approaching her father's house. She is not owned nor even expected. She is a Christmas present, the present of Daddy's little girl.

Brooke steps off the bus in Grand Falls holding a small black purse with two thousand dollars in cash. She wears a grey sweatsuit with the hood pulled up and a puffy black jacket over that. She smells the cold air and it smells familiar. It smells of Michigan winter and frost.

She considers taking a cab but instead walks down the street, the snow crunching beneath her feet. A dog sits on the ground in front of the record store. A boy and his mother walking their own dog come by. The dogs sniff each other. The boy holds the leash. He says, "C'mon Trixie, it's time to go." The dog ignores the child and the little boy looks to his mother for guidance and she smiles kindly. Then she looks at

Brooke and smiles and Brooke smiles back. "C'mon Trixie." The dogs have circled each other, their leashes twined together. One dog licks the other dog's face and the dog yelps and snaps its teeth. They jump two spaces away from each other then move toward one another again. Still sniffing, still curious.

"That's enough, Trixie," the mother says untangling the dogs' leashes. "It's time to go home." She takes the leash from the boy and the mother and her child and his dog walk away, child pleading, "But I want to hold the leash, Mommy. I want to hold the leash."

Brooke stops at the record store and buys a CD. She likes the Pixies. She likes Nick Cave. She passes a fire station that has been converted into a theater and is putting on a play called *Barebacking*. She decides she will ask her father to take her to see it. It could be the beginning of a new career for her. She could be an actress.

She walks for a long time. She walks through run-down neighborhoods and residential areas, Main Street and Bingham Park, named after a police officer who was killed in the line of duty seventeen years ago. Her father used to tease her saying that if the officer hadn't died that year they were going to name the park after Brooke. Brooke Park.

She stops for a cup of coffee at the Cafe On The Park. It's Sunday and inside the cafe people are reading newspapers and sipping warm drinks. She orders a coffee and sits in the corner by the window. A group of high school kids sits on the other side of the cafe and they whisper and they point. Brooke is tired. She feels like she may never have been this tired before. She is exhausted. The bus ride took eight hours. She has been walking in the cold for three more. The coffee doesn't help. It suddenly occurs to her that she is going to call her father and maybe she has come back too soon. She sips her coffee and stares at the payphone hanging on the wall. She recognizes one of the girls pointing at her. It is a girl she used to play with, when she was younger. The girl is pointing and whispering something to a friend. Brooke turns away.

Mr. Haas plants flowers in the yard in the summer and runs in the mornings before he goes to work. Mr. Haas drinks fruit shakes filled with protein powders. He eats salads with low-fat dressing. Mr. Haas wears well-tailored suits and sits in on high-powered meetings. Mr. Haas is the senior partner for the largest law firm in Grand Falls, Michigan. Mr. Haas owns property, plays golf, makes deals. Though fifty-five Mr. Haas looks like a much younger man. His cheeks are clean and fresh. He has a wife who has gone insane. He has long, thin legs. In law school his friends called him Spider.

Mr. Haas believes in hard work and education. He wakes up at 6 a.m. every day to exercise. By 8:30 he is in the office. When he gets home early enough he sits in his library and reads law and philosophy books. Mr. Haas always supports the strongest Republican candidate. He says the poor got that way by choice. He hires junior attorneys from the University of Michigan, his alma mater. They look up to him like he is a god. When they work hard late at night he comes behind them and puts a fatherly hand on their shoulders. He reminds them that hard work always pays off, that life is work, and that loving work is the same as loving life; it is the key to happiness.

People say he has a distinguished face, long and angular. People say he looks like the man you want to be your father, light brown hair, thick and wavy. He can be seen at the opera and the ballet. He sits on half a dozen charitable boards including the one for the Department of Education. He believes in educational reform. He does not believe in blaming children. He insists they know how to read before they are allowed to pass the first grade. Otherwise the schools are penalized. People say he expects too much from minorities, from the poor who don't have the same resources. He replies that he is colorblind. That everyone has the same opportunities. Some people just work harder than others. He will not tolerate crime. He donates generously to support bills punishing criminals. He believes in three strikes you're out. He believes in an eye for an eye. He believes in locking up all the criminals, the thieves, the junkies, and throwing away the key. He believes in prevention until the crime has been committed and then he believes that the community has to take a scalpel to its own cancer and remove the disease.

Mr. Haas has a wife who sits on a large chair in the living room and watches soap operas all day long. Mrs. Haas has big eyes and never seems to blink. A maid comes every day and picks up around the large house that is really a mansion. Mrs. Haas doesn't make any mess except for the crumbs from the potato chips she eats. Mrs. Haas hasn't been out in public in five years. Sometimes she yells at the maid and sometimes the maid hears her and sometimes the maid isn't there. She has lost her good looks. Thirty-three years ago she was homecoming queen. Thirty years ago she stood on the float for her university. She won a beauty pageant when she was sixteen, twenty and again when she was twenty-six. Now her face falls from her bones and her hair has thinned in patches. Large circles have formed under her eyes. She has a double chin. She only bathes on Tuesdays. She has become so fat she barely moves from her chair.

If anybody saw the way Mr. Haas acts around his wife they would think he had fallen out of love with her. He does not hear her when she talks, when he passes her in the kitchen and she mumbles at the walls. He sleeps in his own room and locks the door at night. Since they never have visitors he has taken down all of the pictures of them together. Sometimes, if there is time, in the morning, he comes up behind the maid and cups her breasts in his hands. She responds by pushing her back into him. She continues to do the dishes, or dust the table, until her dress is up (she always wears a dress, just in case) and his hand is between her legs. Then she spreads her legs just enough and arches her head back and breathes deeply while Mr. Haas moves delicately behind her, grabbing her long black hair in his stately fingers. She pushes back into him and her lips part and he pulls on her skin, pushing, pulling, and panting.

His wife used to insist they fire the maid. "We don't need her. She is too young. I want somebody with more experience. I see how you look at her." Now Mrs. Haas watches television eating potato chips and screaming at the walls. Madness runs in her family.

He does not ask how his wife is doing except as a chore. "Did you cut the grass? How's my wife? Did the garbagemen come today?" People would think he had fallen out of love with his wife but they would be wrong. Mr. Haas never loved his wife.

Mr. Haas has only one love in his life, his little girl. She ran away from home two years ago. She was the kind of girl that teachers always said was smart but lazy. Amazing considering her father's reputation for hard work. His daughter always tested the highest in every class. She was always the prettiest. She left him and her home to explore the world. At the age of fifteen she was already beyond the confines of Grand Falls, Michigan. But he knew she would come back. They had an understanding. They had an agreement. He still has a piece of paper buried in the bottom drawer of his dresser. It is a contract he drew up for her when she was ten years old. It reads, *I, Brooke Haas, will always love my father more than anybody else. No matter what. Signed, Brooke Haas.*

A phone rings in the living room. The fishtank filled with sparkling green and orange fish sits on the shelf behind the television. Mrs. Haas thinks the phone is a bad omen. Mr. Haas sees the phone ringing but his wife grabs it first from the stand by the chair. The phone is cordless, heavy, dark and sleek. She listens for a moment. Mr. Haas watches his wife from the edge of the room. She listens to the phone and then throws the phone at the fishtank and the glass cracks a little along the center and then breaks. The water and the fish pour onto the floor. The fish flop around for a moment on the little coral pebbles and pieces of glass.

"It's for you."

When Mr. Haas picks up his little girl she is standing just inside the door of the cafe with a small black purse on her shoulder. Mr. Haas extends from his car and walks purposely toward her and Brooke smiles for him so that when he gets to her he hugs her and despite his best efforts begins to cry.

They drive down the street in his dark Cadillac. Brooke sits comfortably in the leather seat stretching her legs. Soft orange lights glow warmly behind the closed windows of the bungalows they pass. Brooke reclines her seat a bit and her father looks at her gym shoes. Mr. Haas had hired two detectives. They went to Detroit and New York but brought back no word. But here she is, his daughter.

"Chicago," she says. "I was in Chicago."

Mr. Haas nods. "A cold city." When Brooke doesn't respond he says, "Christmas is in two days."

"That'll be nice."

"What would you like this year?"

"I don't know. I guess I would like some new clothes."

"Don't you have any clothes? Is that all you have, that sweatsuit?"

"Yeah. This is it. All I have is this sweatsuit. I know. Can you believe it?"

"We didn't touch your room. You still have clothes in your bedroom."

"I don't want to wear any of those clothes. They won't fit me." Brooke puts her fingers on the cold car window.

"But you look the same." She does too. Her cheeks are the same. She is still a thin and long-legged little girl with dark brown hair cut in a bob. She could still be fifteen.

"But I'm not the same. I just look the same to you because you haven't seen me in a while. I'm actually entirely different. I can't wear any of those clothes, they just wouldn't fit me at all."

Mr. Haas looks for the years in his daughter's face. "Watch the road, Daddy," she whispers to him and he yanks the wheel sharply to avoid an oncoming car. A soft flurry starts to fall from the sky.

"It's a good thing these come with power steering," he says laughing and pats her leg. Brooke crosses her legs and he pulls his hand away. "So what kind of clothes would you like? I think the department store is still open. We could also send Sheila out to get you clothes in the morning. What do you kids wear these days?" He would buy her anything. She could ask for the world and he would put it on his credit card.

"I would like six sweatsuits in six different colors. That way I would have a different sweatsuit for every day of the week."

"Don't you want skirts and jeans and other clothes?"

"I've decided to only wear sweatsuits from now on. That way if I ever feel like exercising, like going for a run, I can just go. You never know when you will feel like running but if you are already wearing a sweatsuit then you can just run, you can run all the time. And people look at you different, or that is to say, they don't look at you at all. When you wear a sweatsuit nobody looks at you. It's like being invisible. Because if you wear certain things then people are harder to trust. But people who will talk to you when you are wearing a sweatsuit, those are people you can trust."

"So you're going to wear a sweatsuit forever?"

"Daddy, you're so funny," she leans over and kisses his cheek. Mr. Haas is so happy his little girl is home. He is so happy that he decides not to ask her what she has done. He doesn't want to scare her away again. He will ask Sheila to pick up six sweatsuits for Brooke first thing in the morning.

"You're still Daddy's little girl."

"No. You'll see. I'm different."

Brooke's mother waits for them in the living room. Brooke and her father step into the entranceway stomping the snow from the bottoms of their shoes. "It's wonderful to see you again," Mrs. Haas says though her chair is pointed toward the television and she can't see Brooke at all. "What have you been doing with yourself?"

"I've been in Chicago," Brooke responds.

"Have you been in any beauty contests while you were in Chicago?"

"No," Brooke says. "That's not what I did."

"Well, you'll have to tell us what you did, sometime." Mrs. Haas turns her chair so that they are facing. "There's no hurry, of course."

"I don't understand," Brooke says. "I didn't think you'd be here."

"But here I am," Mrs. Haas says. "This is my home."

"It's my home too," Brooke says.

"Of course it is," her mother replies. "Because you're my sweet little girl."

Brooke's room is the same as she left it. She presses on the thick mattress, imported from some specialty shop in San Francisco. The sheets are made from rewoven cotton. Stuffed animals line the shelves. She crawls under the covers and pulls her pillows to her tightly before falling asleep.

In the middle of the night she wakes up and turns the lights on. She hears footsteps in the hallway. She looks at herself in the mirror and thinks of Anthony standing in front of his large mirror. She kisses the mirror thinking of Anthony. She misses Anthony. Anthony was so fucked up. She stares at herself in the mirror and asks herself if she is a woman or a girl. She takes her clothes off and looks at her body. She turns sideways, Brooke is thin. She decides she is a woman. There's no way for her not to be a woman. She knows too much to be a child.

She lies awake with the same stuffed animals she had as a child and her room is immaculate. The maid will keep it clean. There will never be clothes lying on the floor here.

In the morning Brooke stretches her arms and pulls on her jogging pants and gym shoes.

Her father is in the kitchen with a fruit shake and a newspaper. He smiles. She takes his juice from him and has a drink and wipes her mouth with her sleeve. "We should run," she says.

The neighborhood is filled with soft hills and rolling green lawns. A man with white hair runs past them and he waves at Brooke and her father. The neighborhood hasn't changed at all. The streets are empty and clean in the morning. Suburban. Their breath makes white clouds as they run. Brooke tires easily. Mr. Haas slows down for his daughter. A few cars sit in front of the houses. Most are in the driveways or the garage. They run in the park.

"Your mother is not doing well."

"I was hoping she wouldn't be here," Brooke says. "I thought she would be gone. That's why I came back. But she's still here."

"Well, it's not so easy. You know, Brooke, when a member of the family is sick, the rest of the family is obligated to take care of her. That's the basis for the family unit."

Brooke stops running and her father continues on for a moment before realizing he is losing her. He stops and walks back toward her.

"You said you loved me the most." The morning light lands on her cheeks. She places her hands on her side. "You said I could be your girlfriend." Mr. Haas' fingers reach for his little girl's cheeks. Her face is so clean in the morning. "You said it."

She steps backwards, away from him. A malicious idea forms in her head.

"Do you want to know what I did?" She steps away from

him, almost skipping.

"No, Brooke. I don't want to know what you did. I want you to be home and know that you are loved and you are safe."

She spins around. "You know in Chicago I sold my body to businessmen like you." She grabs a leaf from a branch. "They waited for me in hotels by the airport. They gave me money and drinks. Some of the other girls would rip the men off but I never did. I always gave them what they paid for because I didn't think it would be honest to take their money and not give them what they had paid for. I was honest. Isn't that important? I ran an advertisement in the yellow pages. I lived with a boy with teardrops tattooed down his face. You know what that means, don't you? Everybody knows what it means when you have tattoos on your face." She spits the last words to her father and realizes she is angry.

The distance between them is the space between his thumb and her mouth. Brooke is sad. Her eyelids close and the tears stream from behind closed eyes down over her lips. Her father wants to hold her but he missed the chance. Instead he just says, "What can I say to you? I failed as a father. You're home now and we'll make it better." Brooke's tears stream down her cheeks as the days become weeks and the weeks become months.

Sheila cleans Brooke's room and puts away her clothes. She does her laundry, puts her stuffed animals back on the shelf while Brooke lays in her bed and reads comic books. Brooke is bored. "I'm an adult," Brooke says. "I can have adult things." Sheila doesn't respond. "Let's go to a bar together," Brooke says. Sheila runs a rag along the top of the dresser and the side of the shelves. "I have a fake ID."

"What can I do?" Brooke asks Sheila and Sheila responds, "Be a girl."

Brooke sits on the sofa across from her mother. Her mother stares straight ahead at the television set. Sheila has cleaned up the broken fish tank, thrown away the broken glass and the black frame and the dead fish. Brooke's mother stares at the television and Brooke sits to the side of her in an orange sweatsuit. Out of the window large green firs with snow-covered branches reach toward the sill but inside is warm and the large room feels small with the two of them in it. Mrs. Haas taps the side of her chair.

"Brooke," Mrs. Haas says. "Are you going to stay with us?"

Brooke turns to her mother, surprised. "I guess so. For a while."

"You probably have friends back in Chicago, waiting for you."

"Maybe."

"Do you miss them?"

"Some of them."

"A boy. Who was your boyfriend?"

"It wasn't anything serious."

"But you never know."

"I know."

"I was thin when I was a child. I was prettier than you," her mother says. "I won beauty pageants. Everybody loved me."

Brooke looks away from her mother.

"Couldn't make it on your own." Her mother snorts quietly. Her mother's fat fingers rest on the chair arms. Brooke pulls her legs closer to her chest.

"I thought you were dying," Brooke says. "I bet you are. I bet you get so fat that you die."

"He doesn't love you," her mother replies. "You're just a skinny little child. You'll never win a beauty pageant. You don't have what it takes to win a beauty pageant. Sheila! Sheila!!" The maid comes running in thinking there is an emergency. "You see her?" Mrs. Haas says to Brooke. "There's your competition now. There's your competition. You don't have an ass like that. You're just a little girl. You're just a whore. You have a whore's ass. Sheila, turn around. Show Brooke your ass."

Sheila stares at Brooke and Brooke stares at Sheila. Brooke stares hard at the woman's breasts, at her legs. Sheila has darker skin than Brooke, larger breasts, thicker legs. Brooke's mother laughs and pounds her fat hands on the chair making the chair shake.

Brooke turns to her mother. "Nobody ever loved you and you didn't win any contests. Nobody loves ugly people and you're the ugliest person in the world."

"I did win contests, Brooke. I won contests and then I married your father. That was the contest I lost. He'll make you fat and crazy too. He's like that."

Brooke doesn't believe her mother and she gets up and as she passes her mother she says, "I hope you die."

"That's a terrible thing to say," her mother replies. "You shouldn't talk to me that way. Don't you talk to me like that, you bitch."

School starts up after the new year and Brooke's father asks her if she would like to go back. Brooke says that she wouldn't. He asks her if she would like a private tutor and Brooke says OK.

She meets during the day with a boy from the university. He has thick, dark eyebrows and square-rimmed glasses. They run through English, history, and math. The boy tells her she could apply for college if she wanted to go but Brooke says she doesn't think she'd be interested in that. She tells him she'll probably be an actress and the boy says that would be OK. They meet four days a week for a month and one day the boy wraps his hand around her hand while she is writing a sentence. Brooke says, "Maybe you shouldn't come over anymore."

Brooke lies on top of her bed in her underwear and bra. She is passion unfulfilled. She has been reading. And she went to a play at the fieldhouse with local actors from the PTA. Brooke didn't think the play was very good. She saw in the stagebill that all of the actors had other jobs. One was a plumber and one was a secretary. It didn't seem very glamorous to her. Brooke feels her father's quick stares when he stands in the door. She spreads her legs just slightly, just enough.

Mr. Haas says, "It's hard to be successful without an education."

"My tutor was a pervert."

"We can get you a girl tutor."

"I don't want to be successful," she says. "I just want to be a maid. I'll just clean things. I'll keep everything clean. There's nothing wrong with being a maid, is there?"

"No, there is nothing wrong with being a maid. But Brooke, you will never be a maid. You could do whatever you want."

"But what if I've already done everything I wanted to do?"

"Darling, you're too young to have done everything. There's too much to do in life. What if I took the day off and we went to the zoo?"

"No. You should go to work. Work is important." He stands in the doorway of her room and downstairs Mrs. Haas lets out a scream. Then something breaks. Brooke covers her ears then raises her long arms over her head to stretch her body. "Look how thin I am. I'm thin. See my stomach? What are you thinking about, Daddy?"

"Brooke. I think we should talk." He sits down on the bed and she moves down toward him. She lays one bare foot on his leg. He takes the bottom of her leg in his hand, runs his thumb over her shin and ankle. "Brooke, I don't think that we've always been appropriate. I want what's best for you. I think that maybe you have read something into our relationship that isn't there."

"Oh," Brooke says turning her head to the wall. "I thought you said I could be your girlfriend."

"That was just a game, Brooke."

"Maybe we should have played Monopoly instead."

"Let's talk about what's best for you." Mr. Haas squeezes Brooke's ankle. "You've been back two months and I know you're still adjusting."

"What's best for me then?"

"Well, we're in the process of figuring that out. But school is best for you. Your family is best for you. Maybe you'd like to speak with a counselor."

"Are you sleeping with the maid?"

Mr. Haas ignores the question. "We need to have a more appropriate relationship."

"For who?" Mr. Haas doesn't answer. "I'd like to know about you and Sheila, you should be able to talk to me about that. Do you want to fuck me, Daddy?" Mr. Haas pushes Brooke's leg away, stands up, retreats to the door.

Brooke stares at him. Asks him to come back. Pushes her hair from her eyes and smiles a short, seductive smile.

"You're growing up. We've made some mistakes."

"Do you think I am plucked fruit?"

"I think you are a little girl."

"A lot of people think I know a lot of things for my age. I'm smart, remember."

"Of course you are."

"Do you want to call me names?"

"What?"

"Do you want me to spank you? Some of my clients liked that. It's really surprising how many people like that. Want to be hit or tied up or something. Don't you think that's weird? I always thought it was so weird but everybody seems to like it. You'd be amazed at the things people asked me to do. I even had clients call me mommy. And I'm only seventeen."

Mr. Haas presses his hands together then runs one hand through his hair. "You're going to go to school. You're not going to sit around the house in your sweatsuit."

"I'm not wearing my sweatsuit now." She rolls over onto her stomach, arches her back, sucks on the tip of her thumb. "Is that how you like it? I'm OK with that. I'll just lie here. I won't say a word."

"Dammit Brooke!" Mr. Haas smacks the wall with his open hand and one of Brooke's stuffed animals falls from the shelf. Mr. Haas places his knuckle against his teeth. "You don't need to do that."

"You should pick that up," Brooke says. "If you love me."

Mr. Haas stands motionless. He looks at his girl's white

skin. All of it is smooth and consistent, like a snow bank. Mr. Haas feels himself losing control. The Brooke that is not a child anymore notices his eyes. She says, "But you want to, don't you?" She looks back over her own legs.

"Yes I want to. But I'm not going to."

Brooke yanks her blanket up and all of her skin to her neck disappears beneath the quilt. "You're just a sick old pervert like all my other clients." Brooke buries her face in the pillow and covers her head with her arms.

"Brooke." She doesn't answer him. He is just a dirty old man in a hotel room by O'Hare Airport. That's all he is.

Mr. Haas leaves Brooke lying in her bed in her sparkling room. Stepping out he nearly bumps into Sheila.

"You wanted to remember this," she says handing him his briefcase.

"Yes. Thank you." He takes it from her and grips the handle tightly.

"I could also be very young," Sheila says. Mr. Haas steps past her and down the stairs.

Mr. Haas thinks about his girl in her underwear on top of her bed and nearly has an accident on the way to work.

The receptionist hands Mr. Haas an envelope and he takes it with him into his office and shuts the door. Mr. Haas keeps his desk clean, a large oak desk that stretches half the width of the office and is shaped as an L. In front of the desk stands a glass table with four chairs around it. Behind the desk large bay windows look out over the city of Grand Falls, Michigan. And if he lets it the sun washes over him half of the day. The office always smells of new leather.

Grand Falls is a nice town. Over 200,000 people live there. There is a zoo and a shopping district. A river cuts across the center and to the north there is hiking and parks and a waterfall. Most of the crime in the city occurs on the East Side. It is the poorest area of the town with a thriving crystal meth trade supported by truckers passing through to Chicago and larger gangs from Detroit looking to produce off the home turf. Mr. Haas cannot see the East Side from his office. From his window he sees an ocean of green.

Mr. Haas sets the envelope down on the glass table. The black phone on his desk flashes a red message light. He takes off his jacket and hangs it up. He sits on his black chair. Somebody made sure that Mr. Haas has the nicest chair in the office. The receptionist raps gently on the door and Mr. Haas decides not to answer her. The receptionist goes away and the silence sounds like sad music. He rings the receptionist. "Darla, could you get me a radio for my office?"

"What kind of radio, Mr. Haas?"

"Oh, something small." He hangs up the phone.

There is another knock on the door. He doesn't answer. His partner Jeremiah pokes his head in the door. "Frank, you ready for our meeting with Siemens?"

Mr. Haas gathers himself together and a smile spreads from his nose to his ears. "I am ready. Of course. I'll be there in five minutes."

"Great. Hey Frank, you feeling OK?"

"Sure. There's a flu going around. I might be coming under the weather a little, nothing to worry about."

"Gotta stay away from that."

"Yeah. Guess I caught it anyway."

"Well, feel better. See you in the meeting."

Mr. Haas sits back in his chair and the chair reclines. He stares at the greens on the trees outside of his window and he thinks about his little girl until another rap comes tapping across his door.

The meeting room holds a large, dark wooden table. Mr. Haas and Jeremiah sit down to speak with two men in dark blue suits. They talk about real estate in the city of Grand Falls and the possibility of a campus being built. Mr. Haas says he thinks it would be a great opportunity for the city and one of the men replies, "And a lot of money for you."

They all laugh. They talk casually for hours. Receptionists and assistants and interns come in carrying coffee and water and sandwiches and cookies. The food stacks up on the counter at the end of the room. All of the men are thin.

When the meeting is over Mr. Haas goes back to his office. He puts his hands behind his head and leans back in the chair and stays that way, humming slightly to himself.

It's night and Brooke is lying with a paperback when a shadow passes under the door. She's wearing her sweatsuit, fresh from running. She's been going further and further. Today she made it all the way to the park and then around up to the schoolhouse. She kept going past the grade school and the firehouse, maybe eight miles total. But she doesn't feel tired. Just restless. Brooke speaks to the walls while the footsteps go back and forth, "I know you're there." Her father opens the door to her room. He stands in front of her, his tie undone, his wrinkled shirt out of his pants, with a small drink in his hand. Mr. Haas never drinks very much. He looks like a man come undone. "What did you do at work today Daddy? What did you think about?"

"I thought about you." He takes a sip from his drink, pulls on the collar of his shirt.

"What are you drinking, Daddy? Can I have one?"

He stalls for a moment, staring at his daughter. "Are you sure?"

"Yes." Brooke pushes her lips out. "I'm used to having a drink once in a while."

Her father returns shortly with a small tumbler with two pieces of ice and a little bit of gin for Brooke. "I had a meeting with some men from a company four times as large as our city. They want to build a campus here. Big companies do small things sometimes. They have to in order to survive. Or at least they think they do." He leans against Brooke's dresser and she pushes herself back against the wall.

"Tell me about it," she says. "Tell me a story, Daddy."

"Do you know anything about emerging technologies, Brooke?" Brooke shakes her head, her mouth pressed against the glass. "Well, most people don't. Emerging technologies are the idea of being ahead of the game, having a system in place that recognizes new opportunities, counters new challenges. The CDs you listen to now were emerging technologies just a few years ago. There's always someone looking to take you down a peg." He sips his drink and sucks the gin off his upper lip. "Oh hell. It's a business term. It doesn't mean anything. Nobody cares about it except people without anything worth caring about. I wasn't really in that meeting. I was there but I wasn't. I couldn't get focused. I told them I was feeling a little bit ill. People are allowed to get ill. I think I might have built up a lifetime of sick days." He laughs a small, tired laugh. "You know, I have never once in my life called in sick. Of course now, I wouldn't have to call in, I just wouldn't show up." He stares absently toward Brooke.

"Do you like the way the room smells? I bought gardenias and lilacs today."

He looks toward the bookshelves and sees that Brooke

did in fact buy flowers. The lilacs stretch toward the windows. The gardenias float in a jar full of water. And the room does smell pleasant. Mr. Haas reaches for his little girl.

"I seem to be infatuated with you. Isn't that odd?"

"I have that effect on people." Brooke smiles and also shakes her head.

Thin white fingers place a small glass next to some flowers on a shelf. Rules are broken. The flowers watch the stuffed animals and the dresser watches the walls. The shades are pulled on the windows. Mr. Haas drowns in a deep blue sea of his little girl and Brooke thinks methodically over what to do next.

13

LANCE SPENDS a long winter lost in the Wasteland, his soul ripped from his stomach, searching out revenge. His tendency toward self-destruction led him there.

People make trips to the Wasteland to buy heroin and crack rocks. Sometimes they go home happy and sometimes they get beat up and their money gets taken. The Wasteland offers no laws and no guarantees. The only new buildings are government buildings, post offices surrounded by barbed-wire fence, fire departments. Ambulances come into the Wasteland and carry the gunshot victims out to Cook County Hospital just outside of the Wasteland. There could never be a hospital inside the Wasteland. All of the Wasteland is sick and dying. The Wasteland is patches of dirt where nothing grows, abandoned buildings full of dying junkies, their veins ripped open, squeezing tight for juice. The Wasteland is a land of flickering light bulbs, unsure pipes, and no place to raise a child.

Lance enters the Wasteland in the winter, his long hair trailing down his back. He cuts his hair off with a pocket knife, sawing at it like a piece of wood, and then tosses it behind a tree stump. He finds shelter in an abandoned building with boarded-up windows. He finds a space on the floor with the other men, women and children. Nobody pays him any attention. He crawls up there and he goes to sleep. And when he sleeps he dreams of Brooke's arms, he dreams of Brooke's love. Every night he dreams of Brooke.

In the daytime he wanders the streets. The Wasteland is

empty. People walk through the Wasteland forever and never leave. The Wasteland is endless. When he is hungry, which isn't often, he lines up at the soup kitchen. The soup kitchen comes in white vans and faceless men in paper masks hand out cardboard bowls full of meat and beans and then drive away. One day a boy kicks his legs out from under him and he lands face down in the snow. Hands fall upon him searching his jacket and his pockets for money and cigarettes. When they don't find any the feet come, kicking him, raining blows.

Men come into the cold building where Lance stays with machine guns on their shoulders. The men wear red and black jackets, sunglasses. They hand out white packets full of heroin. Ten packets per person. The residents bring back money for nine, the tenth they sell or shoot. The residents are given needles. They are told they can leave the program at any time. "Just fill out a waiver," one man says and the others laugh, their machine guns shaking on their shoulders.

Lance walks the naked streets of the Wasteland and cars drive through. White kids from the North Side, from the suburbs, drive up alongside Lance. They never mistake Lance for one of their own. Lance is one of the few white people in heavily segregated Chicago to become part of the Wasteland. He sells nine bags a day and he shoots one at night, and his eyes roll up in his head and he lays on the cold wooden floor with the other residents. They roll around, all of them like demons trying to escape the fires of hell. And then the men come back with machine guns and go through their pockets and take what is theirs and one time the men with machine guns take a man outside and shoot him because the man had made the mistake of doing more than one bag. The people that live in the building are easy to replace. Nobody that lives in the abandoned building is worth more than one bag. Lance shoots dope at night, walks the cold streets of the Wasteland in winter thinking of Brooke, seething with anger. Lance curls up on the floor while Brooke flashes through his mind in clips, her face, her legs.

Lance works the Wasteland and the Wasteland puts years upon Lance's face. Lance sees the man he is looking for working the corner by Garfield Park. JJ drops small plastic bags full of rock into eager hands, he whistles peacefully to himself. What Lance wants to do is easy enough. He follows JJ into the park. Garfield Park is the beacon of the Wasteland, large and green with big cement statues and trash blowing beneath the benches and across the lawn. JJ walks through Garfield Park, where anything can happen. Lance wraps his forearm around JJ's thick neck and he sticks a screwdriver deep in the big man's back, puncturing his lung. JJ falls to the ground and Lance kicks him in the face. "Who's your bitch? Who's your pretty bitch?" he says kicking JJ in the side while the man chokes on his own blood. "I told you I'd be back. I told you," stepping on JJ's face, stomping him with his boot until the man's face is a soft mass. Lance leaves JJ bleeding to death on the cold ground and walks back to his abandoned building where he shoots a bag and rolls around on the floor. People die in the Wasteland all the time.

Lance works out the winter in the Wasteland. A man gives him a small bottle of ink and he uses an old syringe to paint a new teardrop tattoo under his eye. He waits out his anger. Sometimes people tell jokes, rolling around on the floor at night, a joke someone heard escapes from the doped-up darkness. Sometimes people speak of something that went wrong, way back when. They speak of funerals for cousins. They speak of the El Rukns and the Vice Lords, the Gaylords and the Black Gangster Disciples. Life goes on in the Wasteland same as everywhere else, just worse.

As the winter comes to a close the ice and snow begin to melt and the streets are wet. Men come to visit Lance. Friends of the men with machine guns. They come together and they take Lance outside.

"You are one funny motherfucker," one of them says laughing. He is a big, serious man. He is bigger and more serious than the others and when he laughs it is a big serious laugh. They all laugh when the serious man laughs. Lance laughs too. "You gotta be the only white motherfucker on the West Side. Ain't you got a mom telling you not to go into the Wasteland? Look at this scrawny white kid, hanging out in the Wasteland." The other men nod in agreement. The big man wears big black boots and a stream runs beneath them in the gutter from the melting snow. "Listen white boy, it's time for you to get out and get real. Find yourself a white bitch and get your ass a home in the suburbs. Get a job. Put your kids in some private school. When they make enough money send them down here and pick up on some house specialties. You hear what I'm saying. Go have yourself some rich white kids. You'll be bringing heat into the Wasteland staying here. We ain't trying to put this place on the map. The Wasteland is a business, kid. Not some play-ground to run away to."

"Yeah," one of the other men says. "You can't run away here."

"So here's a little parting gift for you. Just to say no hard feelings." The big man stuffs a few bags into Lance's pocket, catching the edge of the material in his fingers, and a big smile grows across Lance's face. "Now go, before I change my mind about something."

Lance starts to walk and someone grabs him from behind and quickly wraps his arms up behind his back. His legs kick and he howls, "Noooooo!" A thick, dry hand holds his face, someone else grabs his flailing legs.

"Oh, I almost forgot," the big man says. "You stuck a screwdriver in my cousin's back." Lance feels the knife's sharpened blade running from the corner of his mouth to his ear and then he falls to the ground. It seems a long way to go. "Smile for the picture, kid."

"This here's a business." Then there is laughing, then there are tires, then there is nothing.

Lance lays on the cold cement, blood pouring from his face. He can feel the wound, a gaping slash along the side of his face. He reaches into his pocket and pulls out a bag. He holds it up near his face, trying not to cover it in blood. He opens the bag and pours it into his hand and snorts it up and starts to feel a little better. Hours later an ambulance carries him out of the Wasteland to Cook County General Hospital.

Chicago makes up for its lack of mountains with an enormous range of buildings Downtown along the lake. The splendor of the black buildings erupting from the city center along the waterfront is as spectacular as anything God planned in nature. In Chicago, man has beaten God at his own game.

Lance drinks a cup of coffee and eats a bowl of chili in a small cafe Downtown. Men hurry in quickly, dressed in brown suits, worried about the stock market. The stock market is crashing. The men curse their fate over black coffee. Women with mean faces come in wearing skirts and nylons eager to get some coffee and get back to work. Then other women come in wearing baggy, cheap pants and men come in blue nylon jackets from the basements of the large buildings. Lance eats his chili and the men and the women all look away from him. His scar is hard to look at. It is as if he had an extra mouth, turned half on its side, puffy and pink, stretching across his cheek. It is more than ugly, it is intimidating. With the tears tattooed under his eyes he gives the impression of a monster that doesn't know whether to laugh or to cry.

He doesn't miss his beauty, his good looks. He cut his long hair himself. He never cared about being pretty. He sleeps in shelters and in the shelters they don't care what you look like. The shelters are filled with men with nappy hair, flies crawling through their old clothes. When he stands by the train station asking for money nobody cares what he is going to use the money for. Nobody tells him to get a job. They just look away and drop quarters into his waiting palm. He spends the money on liquor and drugs and sometimes on food or bus rides.

Lance walks down Halsted and he spies on Anthony. One time Anthony drops his keys while crossing the street and doesn't notice. Lance picks up the keys and follows Anthony to Berlin. When Anthony goes inside Lance places the keys on the ledge near the door so that Anthony will find them when he comes out. Lance watches the boarding house. The shelters are filled with men like Lance.

One day he goes into the Stolen Pony and asks for his job back. Henry cries when he sees Lance and holds him close to his chest. Henry's hands massage Lance's neck and shoulders. "I have nothing for you, my child." He takes Lance's head in his enormous hand and turns it to look better at the scar. He leans his large head in close for a better view, sniffs Lance's face. "I have nothing for you," Henry repeats, handing Lance a full bottle of whiskey which Lance takes and holds onto. "Nothing now and forever."

14.

HALSTED GOES mad for Christmas. The streets erupt with a flurry of trannies dressed as Mrs. Claus, boys searching for some holiday cheer and young professionals shopping for that perfect gift. Anthony walks away from Halsted Street disgusted. Anthony hates Christmas.

For Christmas Anthony visits a hooker on Lake Street by the Henry Horner projects. He feels desperate and alone and more bored than usual. The snow whips through the streets of Chicago piling up in hills and burying the cars on Sheridan near the lake in Roger's Park. The boys on Halsted have all gone inside hallways and parked cars. They went underground to Lower Wacker Drive and sleep in loading docks under thick blankets on mattresses dragged from abandoned warehouses.

Bundled under scarves and a thick jacket and three pairs of jeans Anthony walks below the tracks at Lake Street. She waits for him there, a cheerleader for the trains passing by overhead. The trains rumble over Lake Street like green electric earthquakes and the hookers put on halftime shows in the summer, standing on one another's shoulders, waving their arms and jumping high into the air before landing in one another's arms. They dance for the passing taxicabs as well. In the winter the hookers follow the boys on Halsted to the underground or they bundle by broken stoves in the Henry Horner projects. A train rumbles by, spilling snow on Anthony's shoulders.

She wears six-inch plastic heels and leaves doe marks in the snow as she staggers along below the Lake Street

Elevated. They both have their hands deep in their pockets as the cold city freezes their bones. *What's your story little boy? What does it mean to love you?*

They look at each other, their chins buried in the collars of their jackets. A whisk of snow follows a beaten-down Ford. "Do you want to play?" she asks.

"Sure."

"My name's Candy."

"Can I call you Jane?"

"You can call me anything you want, sugar."

They walk silently, arms locked together to the Henry Horner Homes. Climbing the old stairs among the hum and crackle of burning pipes, they inhale the reek of shit and urine. The lights don't work. The elevators don't work. A man lies face down on the landing and Anthony touches the man's shoulder with his shoe.

Candy takes him to a small sulphur-smelling room on the fourth floor. She runs her hand over his head. He lies down and she lies down next to him. She puts her hand between his legs. He reaches into his pocket and hands her twenty dollars. She looks at the money and then back to him. "Do you like to party," she asks.

"Sometimes."

"Might as well do this first." Quickly she is on top of him, light, more bone than skin, and for a second Anthony is afraid he is going to have sex with a skeleton, then she is up and out of the room. He waits on the bed for her to come back with big men and beat him senseless and leave him to die outside in the snow. He lies on the mattress with an arm behind his head and then he decides to rummage through her possessions. He finds cheap bracelets, condoms, pieces of tin foil.

Candy squeezes back through the slit in the door and Anthony spies a man standing just outside in the hallway. She sits back down and grabs Anthony's crotch then reaches under the bed for a broken tire gauge. She stuffs a rock into the gauge and lights it with a thick wooden match. The smoke boils over the thin metal container and runs up the sides of her face like demon whiskers. Done, she turns to Anthony and smiles. "You want a hit?"

"No. That's OK. I'm just passing through."

"You're a real man," she says. "I can tell." She pulls her skirt up and stretches her leg up to the ceiling. "Don't you want some of this?" Candy rubs between her legs. "I have to stretch because I'm getting old."

You're not getting old, Anthony thinks. You're a crack whore. Crack whores are only two ages, alive and dead. They sit on the bed while Candy smokes her rock and stretches her leg up pointing her heel to the ceiling and the shadow stands out in the hallway the whole time, motionless and ready, like a ghost. Candy peels her nylons off, her skirt. On the bed she is like a skeleton, all of the meat already gone from her bones. "C'mon," the whisper comes to Anthony. "Don't leave me here." He touches her leg, wraps his hand around her thigh.

If I squeezed here, he thinks, I would break her leg. His hand moves up to her stomach and her ribs. A wheezing sound comes from the bed.

"Don't you want to, baby?" Her stick-thin arms are reaching out to Anthony, embracing his neck. "Come get some of what you paid for. Come to *Jane*."

"We never did it with the lights on," he tells her. Candy's skin is dark, almost pitch. "She had blue veins that ran down her legs. She wanted to be an actress. She could pretend to love anybody."

Candy looks to Anthony and Anthony watches her disintegrate into the bed until all that is left is the ash of her bones. Then he opens his eyes and Candy is pulling on her tights.

"You haven't been living here long, have you?" he asks her.

"Long enough baby, but you know, I get around." She smiles toward Anthony. "You're a real man. I can tell. What do you do?"

"I don't do anything."

"You're a real man. We should get married."

"Sure you're not married already?"

"Don't worry about that baby. I get around. You ever feel lonely you come back by. Candy'll take care of you. Doesn't matter, rain or shine."

Exiting the room he passes the ghost in the hallway and he makes his way down the stairs to the cold white streets of the Wasteland. The snow blows along the streets and Anthony consoles himself with the thought, It doesn't snow in Texas.

15.

ANTHONY CLIMBS the stage, again. Stripping is boring. Tonight he works at the Stolen Pony. Stripping even just three nights a week is dull beyond comparison. It's a bad job. You go in you give them one dance for free and they appraise you with their hands. Once you've given something for nothing you can never ask for as much again. The girls at least make good money so they can buy nice things. The boys make much less and live in boarding houses. A few more days and he dances at Berlin. He picked up a shift between films at the Bijou. Lance is not here and Anthony works alone but he is used to being alone. He has adjusted. At least for now. At least until something happens or he kills himself.

C'mon, he thinks. Let's make it tonight. If I can make it tonight there's a chance tomorrow will be OK.

Strippers never get a promotion. Strippers just get old and the skin on their faces starts to sag. They wrinkle. The men go bald and the women lose their shape. Sometimes strippers dance a year or two past their prime because a bar manager doesn't have what it takes to let them go. Those are the darkest years because the stripper goes onstage and gets ignored. Sometimes the men will laugh at an old stripper up on stage shaking her big ass. But it's a catch-22, because the crowd never loved you. They never loved you, they never cared.

Stripping is boring. You go on a stage and the lights play across your body like colored fingers. The music is the same. The smell is the same. If you make enough you make enough. If you don't then you turn tricks, you suck dick, you take it, you take what is given to you. When you don't make enough there's always opportunity to make more. The world is full of opportunities for pretty boys and girls with nothing else to do. Between sets you hang out in cramped dressing rooms, you sip whiskey and stare at the floor.

The music starts and he moves with it while the music moves through him. His shirt goes. His pants go. "Ladies and gentlemen," Henry shouts. "I, your king but also your servant, present for your deepest and darkest pleasure tonight, Anthony in all of his naked glory. Dance for us, Anthony! Dance upon your stage and we will write your book! We will chronicle you with our lust!"

Some songs last forever. Stripping is boring. Stripping is not enough. Anthony comes off the lighted square. He moves through the crowd and dollar bills are crumpled into his waistband. He doesn't care about the money. He is so bored. He needs something, anything, the whole world and nothing. It is not enough. Where is Brooke? Where is Lance? Where are his parents with their Bibles and their prayers? Where is Jane with her blue legs? And what is the difference between all the people he has known and all the people that are here tonight? He has never made an effort to know people. His relationships have always been thin, translucent glass noodles. All the people he has ever known have been the same, like the men in the bar. They are all the same, perfectly interchangeable. He climbs over their laps, the ones that sit on the stools. He hears Henry's voice, "Ladies and gentlemen... Ladies and gentlemen..." He rolls over on his back. He tries not to feel the hands. He tries to keep his eyes closed. He is just an alley cat. He rubs his back across the legs of the stools and the hands tear into him, reach up into his insides.

It ends. The song ends. Everything ends. He pulls his clothes from the floor and steps into the back room and the harsh yellow light. It has never once been enough. Not even close. He has to do something.

The clock radio sings, *We're so vain*, by Anthony's bed.

The spring has come to Halsted Street. Christmas is over and New Year's is forgotten. The resolutions have been drunk away. It's early in the morning and the transvestites are falling out of sequined starlight button-up shirts. Joggers are out, a few of them, running in the streets, singing, *We're so vain*. The transvestites fall from their six-inch platform shoes, sliding like oil from a pan, their bare feet press into the cool sidewalk. They lie face down in tiny puddles next to the gutters in front of the coffee shops.

At the park on Irving a couple plays tennis against the Lake Michigan backdrop. They wear long pants and thick shirts and swing their rackets awkwardly as the wind from the lake carries the balls toward the fence.

Rough Trade prances around the newspaper boxes at Addison and Halsted. Boys with fingers jammed into dark green cami jackets wait out the wind underneath the steel beams. They woke from winter's slumber, addictions intact, skin popping in tiny nervous waves on their cheeks and along the back of their necks. On the first warm day of the year they climbed out of Lower Wacker Drive with chalk under their nails grasping onto the patches of cement to pull themselves up to the surface.

Rough Trade. It's 6 a.m. All the tricks have gone home. The bars closed two hours ago; the men that needed blowing have all been sucked clean behind the dumpsters. The video stores are closed. The boys parade on empty streets under the morning's first light, shivering slightly, lips puckered, fingers stuffed in canvas jackets, the trannies slide from their shoes.

Fashion is important. Today, the *Chicago Tribune Magazine* publishes an article on twenty years of David Bowie, the king of men's fashion. The tall, bony Englishman with the high-pitched voice who masterminded the greatest hits collection *Fame and Fashion*, now available on CD.

Anthony is stuck on Halsted Street. He huffs along his route, having already run six miles, and he stops dead in his tracks. He wipes the sweat from his forehead using his T-shirt as a rag and squeezes his sweat to the ground. He takes the large red stairs at the Belmont station two at a time. He shares the platform with three other people all ignoring each other and waiting for the train. He considers going home to change into something warmer but can't stand the thought of his room. The train comes and Anthony boards with the others and rides the train to Morse. At Morse he waits for the Lunt bus in front of the Heartland Cafe where the pretty waitresses in sundresses serve fruit shakes on the outdoor patio. He gets off the Lunt bus at Washtenaw. The wind chills him. His cotton shirt is still soaked from running and clings to his stomach. The street is a line of townhouses and working-class bungalows.

At Washtenaw and Coyle he is home. The old stucco yellow house is still there. The white magnolia tree is starting to bloom in the yard the way it does every spring, white and pink flowers. The magnolia tree makes Anthony think of paradise. He remembers his mother saying a long time ago, just as they were moving from a tiny apartment east of Clark Street, she said she had always wanted a house with a magnolia tree. She wanted many things. She wanted a maid. She wanted to be left alone. There is a basketball rim up on the garage and the garage door is missing. Beneath his bedroom window the vomit stains have been cleaned.

He knocks on the front door and he waits. Nobody answers. That's the problem with this house, he thinks. Nobody answers the door. He notices a soccer ball sitting near the bushes. He kicks the ball against the stairs and it rolls back to him. He kicks it again. He continues playing with the ball, trying to juggle it on his knee.

In front of him the house is unimpressive, just a yellow stucco house. But the house is large enough for what it needed to do. The street is clean. Anthony almost thinks that he could have been happy here, in this house. He wonders why he ran away but then he remembers.

He leaves the ball and starts to run. He runs down Washtenaw to Boone School on the corner of Pratt. The school has expanded. Classrooms have been built from wood and cover half of the playground. The basketball court is still there. The playground is still there with its rubber floor. At the far end of the asphalt he lost a fight with Felix and Felix broke his leg. He had been defending John Kim. John was a hustler and Felix was a bully but that was just grade school. John shouldn't have stolen the bike. For some reason Anthony got involved. There were others, bigger kids, and there was John. And then Felix threw a wild kick and Anthony's leg was broken.

Anthony sits on the steps and waits for school to start. It's Saturday. Hours pass before some kids come by and start playing basketball. They eye him suspiciously and he eyes them back. The boys divide into two teams to play half-court, three on three. The boys fly gracefully toward the basket. The ball spins from the backboard and through the netless hoop. The ball bounces through their legs. They spin, they try to impress one another. They are young, thin and athletic. They are healthy. When a seventh boy comes along he is told he has to wait, so he sits on the stairs across from Anthony and they watch the game.

Anthony turns to the boy. The boy has a moon-shaped, freckled face and long thin legs like a white popsicle.

On the court one boy throws the ball between his legs and the other boy catches it and effortlessly lays it off the backboard. They shout proclamations of genius and bump chests and slap hands.

The game ends and Anthony and the boy join the others. With four on four they play full court. Anthony is clumsy at first. Older, out of place, over thirty. He hasn't played in years. But his stamina is better than the boys'. He runs up and back, playing both ends. After a few games the boys tire and Anthony takes over. He starts hitting his jumper. He cuts through the lane. He outruns them.

It ends. The boys are tired and Anthony stands with the ball cradled under his arm, red-faced, slick with sweat. One boy knocks the ball away from him, chases the ball down close to the corner of the school. They walk away from the court leaving Anthony wet and red-faced. The breeze is no longer cold. It is just him and the blacktop.

"Give me a dollar, Anthony." Tommy asks Anthony as he pushes out of the Belmont train station. It's a wet spring day and Tommy sits next to a puddle with trash floating along the top, against the Army Surplus storefront.

"Who told you my name?" Anthony says, stopping, staring down at Tommy.

"Give me a dollar first." Tommy's hands are stuffed in his

pockets and he's shivering even though the weather is turning warmer. The cold highlights his white skin against the larger red and purple pimples on his cheeks. He's wearing a Chicago Black Sox hat with a hole in it and a grey scarf around his neck, wet on the ends.

"You're shivering."

"If I had a dollar I would sit inside the donut shop and get warm."

Anthony looks down at Tommy. Tommy looks away and tries to steady himself in front of Anthony. Finally Anthony says, "You're not shivering in a way that gets warm. You've got hypothermia."

Tommy spits. "Fuck you man. You think you can be cool. You're not cool. Give me a dollar or get out of here." Then he spits again, a big bright green wad of phlegm. Anthony kicks Tommy in his thigh and Tommy yelps and moves over. "What the fuck," he says quietly into his jacket.

"You're not tough," Anthony says. "You just talk tough."

"Leave me alone."

"Get up."

"No, man. Leave me alone."

Anthony stands over Tommy who leans away from him over the puddle. "I know about hypothermia," Anthony says. "You wouldn't be the first dead kid I came across on Belmont and Halsted. Now get up." Anthony reaches down and pulls Tommy by his jacket to his feet.

The car hasn't moved in months but it starts on the first turn of the key. Anthony drives south toward Downtown. The Sears Tower watches the big car as it swings toward the lake before veering west. Anthony presses buttons on the dashboard but nothing happens. Tommy hides in his collar.

They pass the Greyhound station on Harrison first but stop short at Cook County General Hospital.

"I was staying in a broom closet, but on Christmas the door was locked so I've been outside since. I hate Christmas," Tommy says. Tommy bites his lip. "None of my friends would let me stay with them." Cook County Hospital looms over them like a giant cement fortress. Tommy shakes his head toward the hospital. "They'll put me in a home," Tommy stares at the large grey concrete building. Ashmarks spread around some of the windows on the upper floors. Some windows are bolted in with fence. "They're going to put me in a group home."

"I know," Anthony nods. "That's what they're going to do all right." Anthony knows about the homes and the alternatives. Anthony knows things don't work, that which doesn't kill you does not make you stronger. Anthony sees gladiator arenas, thirty kids packed to a room, runaways and drop-offs, a handful of staff huddled behind bulletproof glass. The hospital stands in front of them like an enormous gear for some giant machine that tears people to shreds. Anthony knows about the places they put children when they have nowhere else to go.

"I don't want to," Tommy says.

"You're past the point of having a choice."

Tommy squints his face, pushes back into the bench seat with his feet against the dash. He looks about to cry so Anthony waits. "This is going to be terrible," Tommy says shaking his head and Anthony nods because he knows it's true.

"Make a go of it," Anthony says. "If it doesn't work and you still want to die come back to the neighborhood when you're eighteen and I'll kill you myself."

16.

COLIN PUNCHES somebody in the face. The crowd backs up. Colin is a bull. The club is not yet in full swing. Anthony nods to Colin at the door and Colin nods back, rolling his head along his thick shoulders. Anthony steps into Berlin at 11. The bartenders are slinging beers. The kids are dancing and waiting for the pills to kick in. He moves to the back and goes down the stairs to change. Fox is down there going over the stock.

"Fox, can we talk about something?"

"No. I can't talk with you now, Anthony."

"Later?"

"All right. After your shift. Come by the bar."

Anthony changes into a pair of tight black shorts and a silver sequined shirt. He sits on the couch in front of the mirror in the small dressing room. Wrinkles are appearing across his forehead. He squints his eyes, pulls his hair back. If he was anything else perhaps it wouldn't matter so much. "There's no getting past it." He sees a small line of coke left over from someone's binge. "That's rare." He leans forward and snorts it up.

When Anthony ascends the stage it is well past midnight. The crowd is a wave of hands and arms. The air smells of the beginning of civilization. There is nowhere in the world like Berlin, three stories above the highest mountain and not yet conquered. He dances. The DJ spins records, lays a hand on the turntable, and turns around. Someone tries to climb on stage with Anthony and the bouncer grabs him in a headlock and pushes him out through the back door. That person will be blacklisted forever.

Anthony dances for the crowd and the crowd dances with Anthony. He rolls on the ground. He sticks his tongue out and someone places a pill on it and he swallows it. He rolls on his back and someone pours water in his mouth. He swallows the water and he laughs.

Anthony dances and when his set is done he sits bare-legged on the stage and then pushes into the crowd in his underwear. He grabs a girl and she wraps her arms around him and pushes her body against his. They move together. They are liquid, they are joined, his knee against her thigh. He moves away from her. He kisses people. People touch him, he touches them back. The music takes over. Another dancer climbs the stage. Somebody whispers something in Anthony's ear. Somebody whispers they have a limo out front and would he like to go home. Somebody puts money in his underwear. Somebody says, "I have a piece of paper for you to sign." Somebody says, "I want to put you in a commercial. Don't you want to be in a commercial? Why don't you come home? Just come home."

When it's time for his set Fox is behind him on the dance floor. He feels her long hair mixing with his hair against his shoulder. "Get on stage," she tells him. "C'mon now." And he does. He gets on stage and he dances. Anthony can really dance. That's his talent. He dances on the stage and he is beautiful. Lance watches from the back of the room.

Fox watches Anthony reach his peak from behind the bar. She sees thirty-four years of Anthony dancing on a stage, damaged, dancing around, the biggest kid in the club. Everyone in the whole place is on drugs but Anthony is the only one who is obviously on drugs. He seems better with the drugs, less angry. She watches Anthony upon the stage, dancing with his eyes closed, rubbing hands across his nearly naked body, a smile painted across his face. He isn't projecting the hate he normally does that keeps people away from him. She knows it is the drugs and that is why he is nearing the end. She decides she is lucky she doesn't care about boys like Anthony. Sex workers have too much damage. She cares about her doormen and her bouncers, her bartenders and barbacks. But the strippers come and go, there is no hope for them. Damaged goods.

As the night closes and the bouncers are pushing on the crowds with their sticks, Anthony approaches the bar. The drugs are wearing off and he feels tight. He sucks in his cheeks and pouts his lips and Fox says, "No."

Then Anthony begins. "I want to bartend."

"You and the rest of Chicago."

Anthony rubs his neck. "I don't want to be a stripper anymore."

Fox sweeps glasses from the bar. "You are what you are," she says. "Anyway, you get off on the attention. I can tell."

"Yeah, well, I have my issues. But I know. I'm starting to know. I have to stop, it's a dead end."

Fox stops cleaning up long enough to snap, "Life's a dead end. What do you think."

"Look," he snaps back. "What's the big fucking deal. I don't want to dance anymore. What do you care."

"Well, you're not bartending."

"Fine. Give me something else."

"You can work the door. It pays six bucks an hour. I'll see you tomorrow at eight."

"I can't live off of that."

"Sink or swim," she says.

Anthony walks home, unsatisfied. He stops in the convenience store and buys a bottle of water. Six bucks an hour
equals fifty bucks a night. That's not even horse-racing
money, he thinks. At home he kicks the old Caprice before
going inside.

The spring in Chicago is light, and filled with hope. The
kids hang out in front of the Dunkin' Donuts enjoying the
clean, cool sun. One of them asks Anthony for a quarter as
he walks by.

"No, I just took a pay cut."

"C'mon," the kid says. "You got bank."

"No. I'm poor like you."

One of the kids lying against the building pulls out a
knife and plays with it absently. The kid's dirty, homeless fingers grasp the handle. Anthony laughs at the motherless
children and one of them shouts at him, "Hey, fuck you."

Anthony steps in the Stolen Pony. The Stolen Pony has
a way of swallowing light. Placing a lamp on the bar at the
Stolen Pony is like planting a flower in wet cement. The
spring afternoon outside has no effect on the smell inside the
bar. At the end of the bar sits Henry, his large head covered
in darkness like a cap. Henry looks up from the bar, a small
glass of whiskey in his enormous fingers, his large face rolling
over his eyes, falling against his chin.

"You're like one of those dogs the rich people walk on
leashes up the Miracle Mile. The small ones with the
smashed faces."

"There's rich people that would like to own you as well,
Anthony. Why do you disturb me in my hour of peace?" A

dull clunking sound emanates from the back of his throat as he speaks.

"You owe me one hundred and fifty bucks. Thought I'd stop by."

"I owe you." Henry snorts and sips on his glass. "I know about you dancing on that little stage at Berlin. People talk. I know all about you." Henry's voice drips with accusation and self-satisfaction.

"So what."

"We have a contract. You have degraded the good name of this establishment and you are no longer welcome here."

"OK. Now pay me my money."

Henry puts his glass on the bar and stands, his enormous body growing larger as he straightens. "I won't be paying you. It says clearly in your contract that you will not be paid if our covenant is broken."

Anthony thinks for a second of breaking bottles or a window. "You don't even know what a covenant is, you asshole. Your contract is ridiculous."

"Think what you will, I won't be paying you today. Good luck with your new career."

"Sometimes it's cheaper to pay your debts," Anthony says.

"You sound like you have a date with a prison cell," Henry responds. "How unfortunate for you. You boys are all the same. You don't last long. Your friend has been here as well. The one you were so jealous of with those gorgeous markings down his face. Seems he had an accident. He isn't pretty anymore. He wished to climb upon the stage again. Of course, I had to tell him the patrons of the Stolen Pony would not be interested. I have to advocate on behalf of my clients. Your beauty fades as well, Anthony, and then, of course, since you have so little you will have nothing."

Anthony picks up a glass off the bar and drops it to the floor where it breaks.

"Where do you boys go, Anthony? Where do all the pretty boys go when their time is done upon the stage?" There is a flash of light and Anthony is gone and Henry is alone again in his bar with his drink where he belongs.

The doors to Berlin open at 10 every night. Nobody is ever there. By 11 people are pouring in, getting off the train at Belmont, crossing the street from the arcade, fleeing for the gates. By midnight a line stretches down the block.

Anthony stands outside smoking a cigarette and checking IDs. Fox visits him carrying a long, yellow raincoat. "Here, wear this."

Anthony slides into the jacket while Fox holds the shoulders. He feels like a Startrooper, the jacket almost touches his ankles and contrasts brilliantly with the black streets and the green girders. "I am static," he says.

"Keep that," Fox tells him.

"You love me," he replies. "I can tell."

Fox lets out an unsurprised laugh. "What does that mean?"

"What mean?"

"To love you."

Fox disappears back into the club. Her presence is always needed so she is always everywhere at once doing everything that needs to be done, keeping her thin thread of a world alive for one more night.

Anthony continues to check IDs with a flashlight. The kids try to get in with fake licenses and Anthony flicks the cards out into the street. It starts to rain and Anthony pulls up the hood as the street goes wet and shiny and the line gets wet and waits.

At the end of the night Anthony closes the doors to Berlin. The floor is clear except for the bouncers, the barmen, the bartenders, and Fox. The DJ has packed up and gone home. The kids have gone home. Anthony is done and he walks across the sticky black floor and sits down at the bar.

"Can I tell you something, Fox?"

"How long will it take?" She closes the cooler lid.

"It could take a while. I've got a lot to talk about. I've been keeping quiet."

"We can go to Melrose when I'm done."

"How long?"

"Two hours."

Melrose is three doors down from Berlin, a twenty-four-hour heaven. The drag queens stumble in with their dates in tow, boys they picked up at the Vortex or tricks picked up by the White Hen Pantry. Otherwise the trannies come in together, in gaggles of three, laughing and speaking quickly, faces caked in makeup, stubble beginning to poke through. Melrose is a Belmont institution. When everybody is done parading down Halsted in costume at the end of the night, and the drugs are wearing off, they stumble into Melrose for a cup of coffee and a steak. When the kids by the donut shop have bummed enough change they walk in and order soup. When the junkies are coming down from speedballs they order french fries and chocolate shakes. Skinny, blonde college girls strung out on Benzedrine wait on the tables and Anthony orders a coffee.

Anthony nurses his coffee for an hour over the white linoleum table before the waitress tells him he better order some food or split.

"OK," he says. "I'll have a bowl of chicken soup and an omelet."

The food arrives and sits on the table in front of him steaming, and then the steam disappears and it sits in front of him getting cold.

Fox finally arrives and the manager gives her a deep bow. The manager is a short, fat Greek with heavy rings on his fingers. Rumors say that he is connected to the Greek mafia and that he killed a runaway once in the alley for no good reason. He is as feared as anybody on Belmont and he walks Fox to Anthony's table. When he sees all of the cold food sitting in front of Anthony he says, "You don't like our food? What's wrong with you?"

"I'm not hungry. I haven't been hungry in years."

The manager pulls the plates away and the waitress comes around to take Fox's order and Fox says she'll have an orange juice and a water.

"What's on your mind," she asks. Anthony wrinkles his nose and looks around the restaurant.

"What is this place? New Town or Uptown? Lakeview or Boys Town? Wrigleyville, Halsted Street, Belmont Street, you know? How do you put a name on this place?"

Fox sips her water. "Is that what you wanted to talk to me about?"

"No. I just wanted to talk to you." He takes a sip off his coffee.

Fox's fingers trace the tabletop. Her fingers are very long and white. "About what, Anthony? What could you want to talk to me about? I hope you're not looking for a girlfriend because I don't play that role."

"Are you in a hurry?"

"Are we communicating in questions?"

"Do you have to go somewhere? Are you tired? Am I wasting your time?" He tries to smile.

Fox leans back in the booth and stretches her arms over the back of the seat and smiles indulgently. "I have all the time in the world. I never sleep."

Anthony doesn't know whether to believe her or not. He wonders if she is patronizing him. He feels glad that there are no televisions in Melrose the way there are in some diners, but he finds himself looking over at the one wall which is all mirrors.

"Stop that," Fox tells him. "You work the door now."

"I still dance."

"Not at Berlin. I've taken you off the schedule."

"Why did you do that?"

"It's the door or the stage. Nobody does both."

Now Anthony only has one dance job left, stripping between gay porno films at the Bijou in Old Town. He decides he won't go.

"I don't know if I can get by on my wage at the door."

Fox shrugs her shoulders. She doesn't look around. Instead she stays focused on Anthony. She only gives her full attention when she gives anyone any attention at all. "You've made do with less," she tells him.

"Look. This is not what I wanted to talk to you about. I don't care about money."

"I know you don't care about money, Anthony."

Anthony considers how he is going to tell her every-thing but sees no way to get around the block. "What about you, Fox? Couldn't you tell me something about yourself? Something personal?"

Fox leans forward. "Sure I could, Anthony. It's all personal. I was raised in the suburbs and I had two very sweet parents. I've never been raped. I went to a private high school where we wore uniforms and a good college but not a great college. I'm Catholic. I've never been mugged. I've never spent my last dollar. I've never tried hard drugs. For holidays I still go home to see my parents. We still love each other."

"Do they know what you do?"

"They know I manage a small niteclub."

"Do they understand the niteclub?"

"Nobody understands Berlin."

"There's something else."

"No, Anthony. There isn't. Nothing bad has ever happened to me."

"But you're walking on this thread. You're holding it all together with string. It could all fall apart at any moment."

"We all are. Every small business exists that way. There are twenty businesses on this block that exist in the same way and behind that maybe one man holds the deed on all of it and when he sneezes we're all going to be out of work. You can fall off the platform at any time but that doesn't mean you don't try to catch a train."

As if to punctuate her point a train rumbles across the tracks and the tremors shiver through Melrose. A busboy walks by their table in a red shirt swearing to himself in Spanish.

"Ever been in love?"

Fox ponders the question and a sadness passes across her pleasant features. "No. You?"

"Only once, and with a whore." Fox lets out a laugh and Anthony says, "Just kidding." Anthony stirs his coffee. The first glow of the morning shows across the windows as the night goes from black to grey.

"Do you feel better? Or do you still want to tell me something?"

Anthony leans back in the booth. "Once," Anthony says, "I went to Niagara Falls with a girl that picked me up. Her name was Lisa. It was about four or five years ago. She had come into some joint I was dancing in. Maybe the Eagle down on Clark or it might have been the Vortex up here on Halsted. She wanted me to accompany her to a wedding. She was paying me but I don't remember how much. Basic escort gig."

"I thought you didn't do that."

"How do you know what I do? Anyway, I don't. But once in a while." Anthony shrugs and slips a finger through the coffee mug. "What was crazy was that she was so smart and so beautiful. I didn't know why she needed to pay someone to accompany her all the way out there. She had just finished a program and a friend of hers was getting married, a guy named Lew. And then when we got to Niagara Falls she took a picture of me in front of the falls and she gave it to me. I found that picture the other day. And instead of wondering what happened to Lisa I just stared at the picture and I thought 'how pretty.' I was really pretty. I had this long blonde hair, this waterfall rushing behind me, my arms lay against the wooden bannister." Anthony stops, drinks some coffee. Fox leans over the table. Anthony lowers his hands onto his thighs. "I'm horribly vain. I mean it's terrible, I think about how I look all the time. There's other reasons for it. It's hard to explain. But I didn't think, 'Gee, I wonder how

Lisa is doing.' Or 'how can I get in touch with her.' I just thought that if I could be that pretty all the time then everybody would love me and everything would be OK. But I'm starting to reevaluate that idea."

Fox puts her glass of orange juice down on the table.

At 6 in the morning Anthony feels his way along the patch of light scattered through the entrance. Mr. Gatskill's door is open and the old man snores sitting upright in his chair clutching a small whiskey bottle. Anthony wonders if he has ever slept in the bed. Mr. Gatskill's world exists between his chair, the liquor store, and the bathroom.

Anthony unlocks the door to his room and turns on the light. His bed is made and the mirror stands against the wall. The clock radio sings quietly in the corner. The picture of Niagara Falls lays on top of the dresser.

Anthony presses his face to the mirror, stares into his own eyes. He considers cutting his face. He turns up the music on his clock radio and starts to take his clothes off, slowly. He slips from his shoes. He slides across the floor. He dances in the small room. As his shirt wraps around his elbows, over his shoulders, and behind his back, his hands run along his sides. He dances as best he can to whatever music comes through the radio. He sees in his reflection what his face could look like, scarred, never to worry again. If he cut his face wide open he would never have to wonder what people thought of him. He could be a freak, the end of the battle, if he cut his face wide open. Sometimes when something is on your mind for a long time and then you finally make a decision, you do something, and then you don't feel as bad because all of the years standing in front of two doors have ended. You enter a door. Anthony knows that people make decisions and that one decision can make all of the difference and that people often don't recover from their mistakes. Otherwise, you stand in front of the doors forever, always afraid to go in. Afraid that when you enter one all of the others will shut. Anthony knows that in life little happens, a few pivotal moments, a handful of people passing by like pedestrians walking past a store window filled with television sets. The people have their say. The televisions drone on, the stores are covered in dirty glass. He dances to the radio, shedding his clothes. He looks to himself, tries to imagine what the men are seeing when they see him dance on the stage.

Fully naked and down on all fours he approaches the mirror. Face to face with himself he kisses himself. He pulls away from himself. He looks to himself. He punches his face and the mirror cracks. The cracks cut his reflection to pieces. He feels his knuckles swelling and the blood fills his palm. Standing up he kicks the mirror and it cracks in half and the glass covers his floor. Anthony climbs into his bed and his bed becomes a ship on the ocean, an ark. He stays in the ship above the waves of glass and he waits out the sickness. Below the boat his mother is there and he is very young and she is saying something to him, she is trying to convince him of something, something important. She is talking to him and he is looking away, his mother cannot get Anthony to understand and he is holding onto her leg, for protection, and then she stops trying to talk to Anthony. Following is Anthony at thirteen roaming across America in some strange caravan and the smell of flat fields of corn and when the caravan passes Anthony spies a newspaper article floating in the water. He pulls it out of the water and it is Jane's obituary, the girl with blue veins in her legs. He reads of her death in the deep South Side, what happened to her in the hours and days leading up to the event. The minutes before. He swims with Jane. And then he flips the pages back to the sea and days later when the sickness is gone he climbs down, unshowered, the clock alarm beeping madly, and he cleans the remnants of the ocean from his floor and gets ready to go to work.

17.

WHAT IT means to love you. It is every piece of music, every smell in every kitchen. It is in everything I eat. It runs in the streets during the rains. It's the dirt on the windows, the voice through the telephone lines. I took a taxi at night. I was alone and the world was alone with me. I drove through a deserted city looking for a strand of your hair. You are a fire that burns me always. You are my pain, my joy. Every other thought is small compared to the story of us which is the story that defines who I am. When I run I run toward you. All other memories become small bruises, insignificant events. And when you are gone you stay between my body and the warmth of the blankets on my bed. Without you I am always cold.

What it means to love you. Every person that doesn't love you is an insult, an invalidation of you. They bite you, hiss at you, curse you in your sleep. They are against you. Every person that doesn't love you has set the bar too high for you, written a test you can't pass, handed back a failing grade. Demoted you, ignored you, fired you, kicked you out of the family. You are invisible, meaningless, a combination of small events. You are not hated, you are not known. Every person that doesn't love you hurts you, takes away from you, steals from you, stabs you. And there are no kisses, only vision and the rain.

Brooke leaves her father and mother in the living room of their big, clean house on the first day of summer. Her father sits across from his wife who hums to herself pleasantly. Mr. Haas is sleepless, unshaven. He isn't going for a run, he isn't going to work, and the maid isn't coming in. Mr.

Haas doesn't ask Brooke where she is going but if he had she would have said, "I can be dirty anywhere."

Brooke's bus moves quickly now that the snow is gone. The Greyhound buses bring runaways in and take runaways out. The Get Home Free program, started in the 1970s, sponsored by a popular senator from the south, allows run-away children to board a Greyhound and go back home to their parents when they are tired of what the world has to offer them outside the safety of their parents' heavy hands. The runaways sit with the convicts freshly released and five dollars in their pockets. They all sit at the back of the buses and smoke cigarettes and talk about times they have had. Small families form in the back of Greyhound buses. Temporary bonds that run excessively strong. The same as the bonds that form in jails or group homes or among the homeless trapped under Wacker Drive during a bad storm. A runaway sits next to Brooke and tells her she was just released from placement and doesn't have any money. She says she is going to Chicago because Detroit hasn't always been good to her. When the bus pulls into the truckstop Brooke buys the girl a hamburger.

The bus docks on Harrison Street. The driver, a heavyset man with patches of sweat under his arms, gets off the bus first to pull the bags from the cargo hold. The people follow and Brooke gets stuck between two men in the aisle. The driver pulls the bags to the cement, his blue polyester pants grabbing his legs.

Walking away from the station Brooke feels the heat of the summer smacking against her jeans and loose cotton shirt. She pulls a pair of black plastic shades from her purse. "Got a quarter?" somebody asks. She doesn't look up to see who it is and she doesn't reach in her bag for change.

Chicago is hot in the summer and thick with humidity. The streets fill up with beer cans and paper cups, especially around the Greyhound bus station.

Brooke decides she will go to the beach soon, go swimming. Maybe lay out and get a tan. From now on she will not be lazy. She will get things done. Her head fills with plans for a bright and shining future and a smile cracks across her cheeks. She climbs up the stairs and boards the train to Belmont. The train barrels through the city, past the large buildings. As the train leaves Downtown the buildings become smaller but are still large and blocky. The buildings are brick, built to last forever, and Chicago is flat, and there are no earthquakes, so the buildings do last forever. Chicago is a functional town that does what is necessary.

Brooke gets off the train and spins past the newspaper vendor to find herself in front of Berlin but it is early in the afternoon and in the early afternoon Berlin is nothing more than four large black windows facing the street. Next to Berlin there is the restaurant and on the other side a pawn store. People mill on the street slowly.

Brooke lights a cigarette. There is a sign up in Melrose, Waitress Wanted. Brooke lets the smoke run through her nose. Melrose is quiet in the middle of the day, just a few men in shirtsleeves sipping on steaming bowls of soup. Melrose makes money when the streets shut down, a nighttime venture. Brooke stands and smokes her cigarette and walks into Melrose. The Greek stands behind the counter.

"I would like to apply for the waitress position," she says to the Greek.

"We don't hire runaways."

"I'm not a runaway. I'm eighteen. I turned eighteen two weeks ago. Look, I have a driver's license." She pushes her license toward him across the glass counter. He picks it up in his thick fingers and looks at it closely, examining the edges to see if it is a fake, then he flips it back to the counter and rips a job application from a book under the cash register. Brooke fills out the application and hands it back.

"Will you hire me now?" she asks.

"No, I don't think so," the Greek replies.

Brooke turns to leave. At the door she turns back and says, "Can I try again next week?"

"Yes," he says. "You may try again next week."

Brooke continues to the Stolen Pony wondering if she will find Anthony or Lance inside. She misses Anthony. She wants to see Anthony and tell him that she is eighteen now, a woman. She passes many reflections of herself in the store windows, each one different based on the color and thickness and shape of the glass, but each one a reflection nontheless. She runs her long pale fingers through her dark brown hair and enters the Stolen Pony.

The Stolen Pony smells the same, heavy wax, dust, beer, men, and cheap cologne. A few men sit at the bar. One, with a thick black handlebar mustache, looks familiar. Henry pours a drink and a thin boy no older than herself with peroxide-blond hair dances on the small lighted stage. The boy has large white eyes and a thin chest. He dances in awkward, jerky movements, bending his elbows and knees sharply out of time. One man bangs loudly on the bar top to let the boy know he is out of step. The boy looks frightened while he unbuttons the fly on his jeans. His shirt is already in a heap on the floor. The boy looks like he was caught shoplifting and had two choices, dance or go to jail.

"Come along, Charles," Henry says. "Don't dillydally."

The men laugh. The boy is a doe stuck in the headlights of an oncoming car. Brooke leans over the bar and stretches five dollars out but Henry ignores her and watches the boy instead.

When Henry does come over Brooke asks for a gin and tonic. Henry pours her drink going easy on the gin and then he takes her money but doesn't give her any change. The boy dances now in a light blue cotton thong and Brooke watches. Brooke has always liked to watch. The boy's muscles line his stomach like pebbles. The boy is innocent but he got caught somewhere, sometime. The boy finishes his dance and Henry says, "Very good my child. You will be a brave knight." The boy grabs his clothes sheepishly from the floor and marches to the back. One of the men at the bar reaches out and pinches the boy's ass and the boy spins around flustered, eyes shocked, then turns and hurries away. Brooke taps her glass.

Henry comes to her, smiling. "I'm afraid you are not welcome here."

"I would like another drink," she says.

"We don't serve prostitutes. We don't serve hookers or whores, streetwalkers. There is no business for you here in my kingdom. There is nothing to see here."

"Where are they?" she asks.

"*They*," he says icily placing his large, plump fingers on the bar and squeezing the old wood so hard that some of the smell of spilled beer wafts up over their faces. "*They* are no longer here. I know who you are talking about. Those disgusting faggots. They are not welcome here either. The one is a mere doorman, his time upon the stage extinguished he has drifted off into obscurity, a cardchecker, a cocksucker, a servant working the door to an inconsequential establishment. He has faded to nothing. He was beautiful for only a moment and I suppose he's happy to have had that. The other, the one you so successfully destroyed, inhabits the underground, only coming out at night, afraid of the light and that the people will see the darkness that is his soul. He lives beneath the streets, a hunted animal foraging for food in trash bins, dousing himself with cheap alcohol. He is a two-faced monster, unsure of whether to laugh or to cry, so he howls out of the side of his face. He was so pretty once as we all know but that wasn't enough for you. Nothing was ever enough for you." Henry stops himself short, breathing heavily, puddles of sweat forming in the valleys in the folds of his forehead, and then leans forward and hisses to Brooke, "Go back to Michigan, you whore." He is so close that the spit from his mouth hits her and she wipes her face with the back of her hand. "Go back to your father and sleep between his fingers and your mother's chest, or go to your cocksucking boyfriends attached at the asshole like Siamese monkeys. Go anywhere but here because here we run a clean establishment, a bright kingdom uncluttered by the likes of you. Go anywhere but here."

Brooke nearly stumbles from the barstool and when she does stand the barstool crashes loudly to the floor. Everyone turns to look at her. She clutches her purse tight against her body and runs her arm across her face again. "I've never seen anyone as full of hate as you," she says.

"But you will," he replies. "You will and it won't be long, not long at all." By Henry's last word Brooke has run out of the dark bar and into the blistering heat and suffocating humidity of Chicago's summer.

Anthony wears cut-off denims, gym shoes and blue

blockers, an undershirt hanging from his belt loop. They sit outside at a cafe. The cars pass down Halsted, followed by the number eight bus, lending their sound and smell to a very sunny noontime. People walk slowly in the hot sun and the stores have all turned off their neon. Brooke touches the lines on Anthony's face, runs her pinkies along the side of his head. "You were ugly when you were a child," Brooke says.

"Worse than you think."

"Was it horrible?" She touches a rough patch on his cheek and imagines enormous boils sprouting all across Anthony's fifteen-year-old face. Anthony shrugs his shoulders. "You're better looking than you were," Brooke says. "I mean, when I left. You're better looking than the last time I saw you. The lines on your face are not as strong. You're less manufactured."

"I stopped dancing. I'm trying not to care how I look."

"That's probably healthy. But you still care, of course. You can't not care. It's not in your nature. Did you miss me while I was gone? Tell me you did."

A lady enters the cafe wearing a sleeveless cashmere vest with her husband in tow. The two of them look around separately for a table but then settle on one together near the back. Anthony doesn't answer her question.

They sit quietly together, like a couple that has been married for ten or twenty years and has nothing left to talk about. Then Brooke laughs. "Why are you so mean, Anthony? What happened to you?" Brooke lifts her croissant from the white china plate and takes a bite.

"I had a bad childhood."

"Lots of people had bad childhoods."

"Then it must be something else."

"Anyway. You're getting better. That's the thing. I can

tell that about you. You are getting better. I can read it in your face. I think that people get better. What do you think?"

"How can you tell? Better than what? What do you think healthy is?"

"Happy. I think happy is healthy."

Anthony shoots a glance at the couple that came in. They've ordered lattes and muffins and chat with each other, newspapers open on their laps.

Brooke and Anthony walk down Addison toward the lake. The sky is big and blue. Brooke clutches a bathing suit she picked up at the Alley on Clark. "I'll do you both for five dollars," a tall man says from the street corner.

"I'd forgotten Chicago a little bit," Brooke says.

"Six months will do that."

They take the tunnel underneath Lake Shore Drive and come up in Buena Vista Park, a rock garden covered by two small hills and two sets of cement stairs leading to the bike path and then the beach. "I'm going to change." Brooke ducks behind a tree and Anthony stands back on the trail. He catches a glimpse of white leg as she unrolls her jeans. When she is done she is only wearing a little two-piece blue and red bikini.

"Captain America," Anthony says and Brooke smiles.

Through trees and a soccer field they come to the lake. Out on the sand Anthony takes his shoes off and lies down. Brooke lies beside him. The waves roll over the sound of rollerblades. "I'm glad you still live in that building. Otherwise I might not have found you. I stopped in the Stolen Pony. He hates you. Why does he hate you so much?"

"Not sure. Can't say we ever really got along. He's a hard

guy to like, Henry, and I guess I am too. That doesn't make for a great match."

"I remember a lot of things about you, being with you again."

Anthony turns onto an elbow. "We weren't together, Brooke. We don't know anything about each other."

"Grand Falls wasn't all I thought it would be. My father was wrong about a lot of things." Brooke cries. The sun dries her tears, leaving white trails down her cheek. "Don't hate me, OK." Brooke runs her index finger under her eye and Anthony takes a deep breath. He turns one way and then the next. His back feels stiff and he tries to stretch out. He bends his head back. Brooke rubs her forearms over her face. "Just don't."

"I don't. Why would you think that?"

"Just don't, OK? You hate everybody." She puts her hand to her head. The sand is warm under her legs and she digs her heels into the drifts. "You're the only person who doesn't make me feel like a prostitute."

Anthony takes a long drink of beach air. The heat is becoming uncomfortable. Brooke covers her face with an arm and continues to cry. Anthony looks toward Lake Michigan. All of that fresh water. "I'm going in." Anthony stands. "I'm going into the lake."

Brooke grabs his ankle as hard as she can with her thin hand. "No you're not. You're staying here until you say something nice."

Anthony pauses for a moment. Brooke digs her nails into his skin. "I don't hate you," he says. Brooke shakes her head. Anthony exhales. He tries again. "And I want what's best for you."

She lets go. Anthony runs off to the water and jumps in.

Brooke sits up to watch him swimming through the waves, then lies down and closes her eyes for a bit. She's glad to be in Chicago again. Nothing spectacular has ever happened in Grand Falls. Grand Falls is a place where people lie about what they're feeling. Grand Falls is one big lie.

She rolls over on her stomach and unclasps the back of her bikini. The sun bakes her back. The warm sand puts Brooke to sleep and she breathes lightly while Anthony splashes through the waves. Brooke dreams of fire, a burning stove, and then a fire consuming the stove and then the house. The fire spreads, it catches all of the parks, all of the trees. It eats the fire station, the police station, it spreads and spreads and then it stops. When Brooke wakes up she turns her head and sees Anthony standing behind her, water falling in drips from his long hair. A cold drop lands on her leg.

"It's good to see you again. For a moment I wasn't sure."

"You were saying things."

"Nothing true, I hope." Brooke lets out a small laugh and rolls onto her back exposing her naked breasts, her bikini top hidden behind her. She stretches her arms up toward Anthony.

"Your back's all red. It's gonna hurt in an hour. You better get some sunscreen."

They walk back and Brooke does stop to buy some sunscreen in the Walgreens. "I guess I'm just too pale to tan. I guess. Look, let's get a drink. I'm dying of thirst."

The evening brings a cool, tropical breeze and they drink gin and tonics on the outdoor patio at Roscoe's. The bartender eyes Anthony while shaking up Cosmopolitans. The bartender imagines what he would do to Anthony given half a chance and when Anthony tries to pay for the drinks the bartender waves him away.

The sun slips behind the buildings leaving a golden glow over the streets. The glow wraps itself around the lampposts. The boys come out on Halsted and Brooke and Anthony watch as they hustle drugs and sell their asses to any car that passes by. The children sulk by, the runaways, hands in pockets, then the college kids, fresh haircuts, clean shaven. They all pass by the patio at Roscoe's on Halsted Street. Anthony looks away. He has seen enough of Halsted for a lifetime. Anthony is glad he doesn't have to work tonight and sips leisurely on his drink.

"Sex," he says.

"Sex."

As the night becomes darker the trannies come out of the doorways and step from the buses. The girls come as well and soon no one can tell. Halsted Street becomes a parade, a flea market.

"Once you've done it, then it changes everything." Brooke feels the liquor and she stirs her glass with her finger. "I didn't think that but now I know." They nurse their drinks and think of how their lives have changed because they have done it.

Climbing the stairs to the boarding house they hear Mr. Gatskill call out, "I knew she'd be back!"

Drunk, the two of them go to Mr. Gatskill's doorway. He sits up in his chair. "Give an old man a kiss." He sits in the same position Brooke left him in, with the perennial bottle in his right hand. Brooke kisses the old man on the top of his head. He hands the bottle to Anthony and Anthony takes a small drink. "You'll spend some time with me now, won't you? I might even turn up the sound on the television if you like." Mr. Gatskill lets out a dry, raspy laugh.

"I don't have anything to do. I'll get a board game," Brooke tells him.

"Board games are good. Or we could play cards. And if that bastard kicks you out you can sleep on my bed. I haven't slept on it in years so it's clean." Mr. Gatskill lets out another laugh.

Anthony leaves Brooke with Mr. Gatskill and takes a shower. When he comes to his room Brooke is lying face down in his bed. "Go shower," he tells her. "You're full of sand."

While Brooke is gone he changes the sheet on his bed and he dresses in a clean pair of shorts. He lays down in the bed, the gin sitting smoothly in his stomach. Knocking sounds come from the ceiling and Brooke climbs in next to him still wet, only wearing a towel. He covers her with the blanket.

"You're not going to kick me out, are you?"

"I don't care if you stay."

"Forever?"

"What is forever?"

"We could get a real apartment. A one-bedroom. With a stereo."

"Don't think so far ahead. I could get knifed in an alley tomorrow."

"I have money. And I'm going to get a job." Anthony snorts. "Not that job. I'm done with that job. When you do that job you stop enjoying certain things."

Brooke lets her towel unravel and surrenders to the blanket. Anthony crosses his arms over his chest and falls asleep.

18.

AT 6 A.M. the lights go on in Mission Church on South State Street. Lance and a hundred others are engulfed in neon wilderness and the smell of industrial antiseptic and oatmeal, overpowering the sour smell of drink and neglect crusted into flannel shirts. The residents stir along the floor, a jumble of snorts and wheezes, rising slowly, pulling their shoes on, packing up their mattresses, stacking them against the wall with their blankets and sheets. Runaways are not allowed in the shelter. Two flat-chested queens with nappy hair push brooms along the linoleum. Two pink-faced young volunteers man the food line. "High school students," Lance laughs when they hand him the white styrofoam bowl, and he grabs his seat at a long wooden table and digs in with the other old men.

The concrete steps into the church are soaked in urine left by the ones that didn't make the cut the night before. Above them the pink neon cross is turned off for the day and Lance moves with the rest of the line aboveground. Outside and across the street the Area One Police Headquarters watches them, a square tanker of a building six stories high and surrounded by barbed wire. A block down State Street a pastrami shack with a Vienna Dogs sign is already open and serving the officers sandwiches and coffee. South, the abandoned buildings beyond Mayor Daley's revitalization program lie in rubble. The Elevated and the subway run as dual currents at State and Roosevelt where the blue and red lines intersect. The homeless scratch their heads and spill off to find their own path for the day.

Lance walks east toward Soldier Field. The sun rises early on Grant Park and the Shedd Aquarium, quickly clearing a grey haze. Lance wipes the sweat from his head with his fist. Near Roosevelt the aqua-green walls stretch into the lake to keep the whales in. The Buckingham Fountain turns on at 10 o'clock. and the tourists take pictures. The lakefront humidity drenches the lunch crowds of the Chicago Loop, washing over the buildings Downtown, splashing against the Sears Tower. As the buildings pour onto the street the streets quickly fill until it is hard to move between noon and one. The cars line up, the horns start to fire, a strong hot wind sweeps in from the east funneling between the buildings, the pedestrians rotate past the cars and through the crosswalks as if on moving tracks.

At the intersection of State and Madison Lance stands with a cup of coffee while the recruiters take a break from the phone banks at Rodriguez Consulting. A lady in a red skirt presses a dollar into his hand. "I'm just standing here," Lance says but the lady is already caught up in the street's fast-moving concrete blocks. Lance passes the famous clock at Marshall Field's. If only it were December then the windows would be filled with Christmas decorations, the edges painted white for snow displaying Santa Claus and warm scarves instead of pale ceramic waifs in striped bikinis. December seems important to Lance.

Lance tromps along the lake path, toward the North Avenue slab, hundreds of feet of cement, a man-made dock overlooking the Ferris wheel at Navy Pier. The Ferris wheel spins in the background. The med students from NU take turns jumping into the lake, lying on the slab like seals with their books open. The students seem to shine, their skin is clean and their hair is full and neatly cut. At Wilson Lance comes to the outcropping of brown rocks symbolizing Uptown. Lance looks for needles floating in the sludge.

Brooke walks in a blur. He never knows if it's a dream or not anymore. Lance wonders if he is on a mat in the State Street Mission when he sees her. He feels in his front pockets. Her short black skirt surrounds her thin legs like electricity. Lance watches her feet on Belmont. Lance pushes his fingers inside his shirt, tracing the bones in his ribs, pushing on them. He follows her past the army surplus. A boy sitting against the glass of a store bumming for change reaches out and grabs the cuff of Lance's pants leg and shakes a finger at Lance. Lance stops and bends down to face the boy, his knuckles resting on the cement.

"You see what I'm doing, huh?" Lance asks and the boy nods. "I'm not crazy," Lance tells the boy.

The boy rubs his hands together as if he had just finished eating something. He looks around him for his friends. "Never said you were."

"You need money?" Lance asks.

"Who doesn't," the boy replies.

Lance reaches into his pocket and finds the dollar and a bus token, which he hands to the boy. The boy squeezes his hand around the money and says thanks, watching Lance closely. Lance hangs in front of the boy, his arms swinging at his sides, smiling in such a way that only the right side of his mouth opens and the boy sees Lance's back teeth.

On the side streets near the boarding houses the trees create a false roof. On the corner of the triangle there is a bright yellow bagel shop across from Penny's Noodles. Lance sees Brooke reach for Anthony's hand at the restaurant and Anthony pull his hand away. Anthony always pulls away. By the pawn shop Lance's footsteps have synchronized with

Anthony so that he is a shadow and can feel Brooke reaching for his wrist. Lance hears his name slide from between Brooke's lips, floating lifelessly toward Anthony in the noisy production beneath the tracks. She's asking Anthony a question. And he sees Anthony's response, Anthony shakes his head and looks away from her.

The north-south trains run all night long. Brooke and Anthony fade into the bricks of apartment buildings. The north-south trains return Lance to Roosevelt Street. At the Mission Church the lights of Belmont are still stretched across Lance's eyes. "I'm a damn good-looking man," one of the residents says stepping loudly through the hall waving a blue and orange Bears hat like a flag, like he was going to lead a revolution straight to the meatpacking plants. It's been ten years since the Chicago Bears won the Super Bowl. "Angel's a good-looking man," he says still waving the hat, daring anybody to try to take it away from him. "That's what she told me."

"If you're so good-looking," Lance says, his lips puckered as if to hum a song, his mat pushed up against the wall so that his ankles lay at the edge and the heels of his shoes touch the floor, and an arm bunched beneath his neck for a pillow, a young volunteer preparing to turn the lights off for the night. "If you're so good-looking what are you doing in Chicago? Why don't you go to Berlin?"

19

THE NIGHT has started. Anthony stands with Colin guarding the front door to Berlin. The line grows and they collect identification cards. Colin makes sport of the door, threatening people, telling them they can't get in. Anthony doesn't care. He checks the ID, takes the money, and shuffles the children past. Inside Berlin there is a boy dancing on the stage in light blue briefs. There's always another boy for the stage. The boy has dark skin and blue eyes, the line on his stomach is deep enough for a river to run through and he dances close to the edge. The boy is older. Anthony has seen him before.

"Sometimes," Colin says to Anthony, "nothing happens here." Colin spits on the sidewalk and wipes his mouth with his big arm. Colin has been working the door at Berlin for three years and speaks to Anthony like a person with experiences, but Anthony isn't much taken with Colin. Anthony has experiences of his own. Colin with his big fat arms and his tattoos and piercings. For Christmas Colin worked the door dressed as an elf. "Sometimes shit blows up. You don't know, brah. Shit just goes crazy. Stay close."

The line at the door grows but inside capacity has been reached. Anthony pokes his head back in the door, the stage is empty, between sets. Fox stands near the back of the bar. He closes the door and there are two large men in suits standing in front of him with briefcases in their hands. Anthony blocks their way. They have removed the velvet rope.

"This is not your crowd," Anthony tells them. The two

men look at each other and laugh.

"He's just kidding," Colin says. "C'mon in." Colin guides the men through the crowd, parting the children. He guides them to Fox who nods. They all talk, Anthony watches from the door, pink lights spinning across the bar. Fox moves her hand and Colin retreats back through the crowd to the door. Fox moves like she is offering something and the men shake their heads like it is not enough. They gesture and smile. A handoff is made. Directions are given.

"It's never enough."

"What the fuck did you do that for?" Colin asks.

"Fuck you."

Colin grabs Anthony's throat in his large hand, the line lets out a collective gasp before being rattled by a train passing overhead. Anthony's face turns red and he can't breathe but he smiles for Colin anyway and Colin lets go, unsure what to do. Lance watches from across the street, hidden behind girders.

"You're a bad mother," Colin says. "I'll give you that, brah. But I'll break every bone in your body you give me a hard time."

"What would Fox say?"

"Yeah, what would she say?" Colin rolls his shoulders. "And who would she say it to?"

Colin and Anthony face each other. Anthony tells him, "She'd say leave her door guys alone. She'd never talk to you again. She'd spit on you. She would never forgive you. Watch yourself." Anthony jabs Colin in the chest with his finger to make his point.

Colin's face falls and he squeezes his fingers into fists as if he were bending steel. He lets it pass over him and finally says, "You're not a dancer anymore."

"Let us in," someone yells.

"Who said that? Who the fuck said that!? You are fucking banned motherfucker. Who fucking said that!?" The line stands quiet; nobody wants to be locked out of their own youth.

The men in the suits come out with their suitcases except now their suitcases have weight. Anthony stares at them hard, hoping to provoke a confrontation, he's feeling like one, but the men just walk away. They don't notice him.

Late at night Anthony is not home from work and Brooke swings her legs off the bed. She cannot sleep and Halsted Street calls her. She leaves the boarding house, stepping quietly down the stairs. She walks down Halsted Street in the artificial glow of the neon lights reflected from emerald lipstick and pastel heels. She wears her blue jeans, and the breeze that blows through her hair is like she is on an island. She likes the thought of an island in a city and plays with it in her mind. She thinks it is going to be a hot summer.

The Treasure Island grocery is closed and all she can make out are the silhouettes of lovers, hookers and Jons. Brooke knows that half the world is made up of hookers and Jons and she laughs because she is wise for a girl her age.

Lance waits for her beneath a streetlight. He leans up against the pole of the light. He breathes in the smell of old paint and steel. He wears a sleeveless shirt, black pants. He holds a knife in his right hand. Brooke enters into the pool of light cast by the streetlight and the light swims around her legs and arms. She looks at Lance and startles for a second, then turns her head away. Two fish in a bowl. She does not see Lance and Lance holds his breath.

"Look at me," Lance whispers to Brooke, the knife cutting into his hand. "I became ugly for you. Look at how you killed me." But the words are silent. They are only thoughts. Lance doesn't have the heart left to broadcast them and Halsted Street doesn't care. Brooke disappears from his view.

Brooke walks Halsted Street. The kids sit on Halsted and Clark. There are always the kids, hanging out in front of Dunkin' Donuts. The runaways hold down the corner. The runaways have a motto, "Three for them, one for us."

It's late at night and the kids sit on the corner in black clothes doing nothing at all. Brooke sits down on the end, next to a blonde-haired girl. The girl turns to Brooke. Her features are slow and sad. The blonde girl has a face that has fallen down around her jawbone. It makes her look very old but her eyes say she is only sixteen. "Do you have any smokes?" the girl asks.

"I could get some," Brooke replies.

At the end of the night Anthony sits at the empty bar having a drink before going home. Brooke will be waiting for him. Anthony drinks slowly and Fox stands in front of him counting out the money. She wears a dark blue sweater and a pair of tight jeans. Anthony contemplates his whiskey. It is late in Chicago.

"What about those men?" Anthony asks. "Why give them anything?"

"Because they own this place."

"They don't own it. You can't own a bunch of freaks strung out on drugs." Then he says, "It's a miserable ending, to give everything away."

Fox stops. "Did you ever notice all of the apartments when you're walking home, all the windows? Do you realize how many people live in this neighborhood? In this city? You worry about a couple of men and a small bar. Two years this place will be gone and maybe there'll be a laundromat here. Men will come with suitcases and clean the quarters out of the machines. Do you care?"

Anthony sips his drink.

"Try to make two people happy and one person miserable. Count yourself." Fox grabs the cash drawer and disappears with it downstairs to the dressing room. Anthony watches Fox go and looks into the rust-colored glass.

Sometimes the world is a raging storm. Anthony chews on the world through the alleys he walks. He rubs his neck which is bruised and sore from Colin's hand, he stretches his arms out as wide as they'll go and pulls them back into his chest. He replays Fox's words. He watches the ground as he walks. He feels the stones and beercaps under his shoes. He nods his head to the music of late-night wind across garbage can lids. He scratches across his chin. Lance's footsteps blur behind. "Nice night for a walk," Lance says, kicking a rock into a trash can. "Little cool, little hot."

Anthony turns to face him. He sees the scars and the tears. They lock eyes and Lance comes really close. Lance is so close that the puffy scar on his face almost touches Anthony's nose.

"I've lost a step," Lance hisses. "I'm not quite as pretty as I used to be."

"Yeah, well... Maybe you should have gone to school and gotten some other skills. Don't want to put all of your eggs in one basket. You know how that one ends."

"Do you know how this one ends?"

"Hey, give it a rest. You threatened to kill me once before, remember."

"I do remember," Lance tells him, looking back over his shoulder, as if somebody else was listening. "I remember everything that has ever happened. I have never forgotten anything." Lance backs away from Anthony, seats himself on top of a trash can. The moonlight casts a mean glow across his face. Most of the world sleeps. "I had an accident." Lance traces the scar along his cheek. His hair cut short as if with a butcher knife. "I fell in love with the wrong girl. Do you know what that means, to be in love?"

"I knew a woman once who was murdered down by the Taylor Homes," Anthony says. "We spent a lot of time together."

Lance picks up a pebble and throws it into the air. A pale yellow light goes on in the building behind him and then turns off. "Listen," Lance says. A wind cruises through the alley but the wind becomes the tires of someone's car and the headlights replace the moon and then the car is gone. Then the wind is an open window. A thief crawling in from the yard. After that the wind is a child silently stepping down the back stairs while the child's parents sleep. "It's the most painful thing," Lance spits. "I've been raped, beat up. I've been stabbed, jumped out of windows. But nothing was ever as bad as that. That was the worst." Lance pushes his palms onto the trash lid then turns his palms up for Anthony to see the streak of blood on the still-open wound.

Lance fumbles in his jacket. A mouse runs past Anthony's foot. Lance pulls out a cigarette, lights it with a long wooden match he strikes along the side of an abandoned brick garage. "Smoke?"

"No."

Lance inhales the smoke but his mind continues to race. Lance turns and in the glare of the cigarette's tip Anthony notices the bottoms of Lance's eyes are yellow and the tops are bloodshot red, like a thunderstorm. He's ill. "So how is she?"

"She's all right. She's asleep in my bed right now."

"I know that."

"I figured you did."

Lance blows the air out of his cheeks in a low whistle. "I tell you, the past few months have been chaotic. I can't capture my thoughts. I'm scattered, you know." The glow from his cigarette illuminates Lance's naked arms, pockmarked and bruised. "You're a pretty bold guy, Anthony. Aren't you afraid of anything? Aren't you afraid of being cut?" Lance runs his finger over his face again. "I was cut, you know."

"Sure I'm afraid of being cut. I'm afraid of everything. My own shadow. What's not to be afraid of? Fuck it. I'm not much of a model for how to deal with the world."

"I hurt, Anthony. I hurt all the time. And I want to see her."

"You feel bad. All that time you were following us. Why didn't you stop us and say hello?"

"Look at me."

"It wouldn't have mattered. She fell out of love with you a long time ago. Even before you were cut from mouth to ear."

Lance pulls thoughtfully on his cigarette, trying to push out rational sentences from his jumbled mind. "But why would she fall out of love with me? I never changed, never once. I told her that. I never once changed."

"What does that have to do with it? She woke up one day and she didn't love you. That was the end of it. Maybe you hit her too many times. One day she walked left instead of right. I don't know. How can I tell you why she stopped loving you. Some people fall out of love, some people don't. Look at your face. Things don't always make sense. Anyway, you don't know anything about love."

Lance lets the smoke run up his nostrils. "I'm going to kill you."

"You can. But you can never get her back. You can kill the whole world. She will never come back. She will never take you back. She will never come back. She doesn't look for you. She doesn't see you."

Lance bangs the trash can lid. Anthony moves toward Lance and stretches over him. Lance's cigarette burns at their feet. Anthony sways slightly, as if there were a song playing quietly behind the garbage bins. Lance shivers in his arms. Anthony holds Lance and Lance buries his horrible face in Anthony's chest. Anthony feels the wet salt of Lance's tears. Lance cries for his mother and for all the years lost to locked institutions. He cries for the Wasteland, he cries for Brooke. Lance cries most of all for Brooke. Lance cries for a long time, fills the alleys of Chicago. He has lost his girl, his only girl, to the city and himself as well. Lance cries for Chicago and he cries more for Brooke. Lance's tears for Brooke have no end. The salt pours down Anthony's chest. Anthony's stomach is soaked in Lance's tears. Anthony feels the steel along his stomach, cutting a line. Anthony's stomach is lined with muscle. He doesn't like to eat. He feels the knife cutting a line along his belly and he feels his blood running over his belt and then the knife is turning, and it's in Anthony's hand. And then the knife is running along Lance's stomach, up, two men fighting, a nick just below Anthony's eye, through Lance's chest. Their blood mixes together, they hold each other as the knife dances between them, arms around each other's necks. They hold each other for life. They squeeze each other. Their blood runs through each other's veins. They become whole the way they said they would if they were together, all of their blood mixing together before finally cutting a long, straight line across Lance's neck and Lance is dead in the alley.

By the time Anthony gets to the Dunkin' Donuts most of the kids are gone, either to Neon Street Shelter where they can get an anonymous bed for two days, or they're hiding in a hallway or a rooftop. Maybe a couple have gone to Alternatives where children are connected with twenty-one-day foster care while the state takes custody proceedings. The kids left are over sixteen or look it or just don't care about the curfew laws for minors in Chicago.

One younger kid sits against the corner block of the building, head lolling to his side, half of his face lit by the pink sign.

"You awake?" Anthony asks him. The kid looks up.

"You're bleeding," he says.

"I am," Anthony replies. Anthony takes off his shirt, torn and stained, touches the cut on his stomach and then dabs at his face with his shirt and sees more blood. "I am bleeding."

The kid hands Anthony a coke bottle filled with water and Anthony pours some on his shirt and uses it to wash some of the blood off. "What's your name?" Anthony asks.

"Jenks," the boy replies. Jenks opens his backpack and pulls out a shirt. "This will probably be tight on you." He hands it to Anthony.

"I'm going to have to get this back to you," Anthony says pulling the shirt over his shoulders, keeping the other one as a wet rag against his eye.

"I got it at the church on Wellington," Jenks says. "They give away clothing over there if you ask for it."

"What else?"

"It's a nun. She gives us things."

Anthony nods. The streets are warm at night in the summer. The easiest time of the year for runaways. He looks down at Jenks who is a good-looking kid, olive skin, a round face. A bull with horns drives by, slows to look at Anthony and Jenks, then continues on around the corner.

"How long have you been coming here?" Anthony asks.

"A little while. On and off." Then Jenks says, "Nothing's open except the Dunkin' Donuts at this time of night."

Anthony feels his head clearing. As it does the cut under his eye starts to sting and the different colored lights become more stark in their contrast. Morning will come soon. "I was wondering about a kid named Tommy," Anthony says.

"Tommy Tommy. Ugly Tommy. He's in Lawrence Hall," Jenks tells him. "That's a temporary shelter. They'll ship him somewhere from there."

Anthony nods. "I know what Lawrence Hall is," Anthony says. "That's a rough place."

They don't say anything and Jenks leans back against the building and moves to get comfortable. "Is there anything I can do for you?" Anthony asks turning from side to side.

"Doesn't look like it," Jenks replies.

"You're a likeable kid. You'll do fine."

Jenks nods. "I'm going to sleep now. Keep the shirt."

The shower runs in the boarding house. Brooke knocks on the door to the bathroom but Anthony doesn't answer. He washes the blood from his hair, from his face. He washes the blood from his stomach. The cut there is perfect, like a cesarean section, as if someone had cut out his baby. The cut is long and thin but not deep. Brooke gives up and retreats to the bedroom. Anthony showers and scrubs for hours, running his fingers through his hair rinsing the soap and rubbing the bar over his body. He rinses his shirt squeezing the blood out onto the shower floor. At first the water is red, then pink, then clear and Anthony can drink it. The cut's not deep. He takes an old towel and scrubs his body with it over and over again, and when Anthony steps out of the shower he is as clean as he has ever been.

Back in the room Brooke sleeps peacefully and Anthony dresses quietly in a black T-shirt in case he starts bleeding again and a pair of jeans. He stuffs the clothes he was wearing into a white plastic bag and leaves.

The morning workers are moving through the city. The store owners are hosing down their sidewalks. Anthony stops at the corner store and buys band-aids, lighter fluid, and a book of matches. He places a band-aid on the cut under his eye. He burns his clothes in the alley. He retraces his steps to Berlin. People are awake and they fill their windows. The alleys are loud with the bang of taking out the trash or throwing the trash down the chute from the third floor, the bottles and cans rattling their way to the bottom.

Anthony stops at a quiet spot in the alley a couple of blocks before Belmont. It was here, he's sure of it. Lance is gone. He looks behind him and ahead. Nothing. The garage to his right opens slowly and Anthony waits as a car slides out and past him and the garage door closes.

Anthony searches around the trash can, kneeling near the fence. There's a dent in the lid. He finds a cigarette butt around the bottom rim but that could belong to anybody.

Anthony spends the day in the library and sleeps in a hotel because he doesn't want to see anybody until he is sure, but then in the morning he looks through every newspaper, combing every page. And when he is done with the last one he looks up at the old men with green hair who spend their days in the library. "It's horrible," he says to them. They turn. The librarian looks up from her book. "Not a word. Not even a mention." The men turn to him for a moment. Crazy people come through the library all the time. Less in the summer. Anthony places the papers back on the rack and goes to work.

Colin and Fox don't say anything about his appearance and around one in the morning Fox approaches him.

"I'm sorry," Anthony tells her. "I'm at a loss."

"You're just tired," she says. "I want you to go home and get some rest and then sleep late tomorrow so you come in tomorrow night feeling better."

Anthony pushes open his door and sees Brooke sleeping in his bed. He climbs in next to her. His stomach stings from the cut. A teardrop has been cut under his eye for the man he killed.

"Remember how beautiful we were, Brooke? We'll look back on these days as the days when we were beautiful, kings and queens of the niteclubs. Remember how they parted for us when we moved from the dance floor to the bar?"

Brooke stirs and turns toward him. The cut under his eye startles her. He peels his shirt off and she sees the line in his stomach. She touches Anthony's face. She sees the teardrop cut and she knows. She touches it gently with her pinky and Anthony closes his eyes. "I was worried when you didn't come home."

Anthony doesn't respond for a bit. He wants to give himself away, like a donation. He wants to be no more of himself. His self-loathing has made him tired. His own hatred has drained him clean.

"Don't cry. I'm going to love you so much that you are never going to need anyone else," she says. "Look," she says nodding toward the window. "The sun is coming up already."

The morning comes for all of the glitter and broken heels on Halsted Street. The buses run again. The stores open. The children in the doorways and broom closets, boiler rooms and youth shelters, collect their belongings and count their change. Some of them consider going home and some consider staying away forever. The sun spills on all of the runaways on Halsted Street and the runaways stretch their legs and rub the sun out of their eyes.

Brooke runs her fingers along the cut on his stomach. "Don't," he tells her. "I don't like it." But Brooke leaves her hand on his stomach. She pushes on him, spreads her fingers along his wound. He covers his face and breathes in the hair on his forearm. Brooke pulls away from him. They try to sleep but Anthony just stares into his arm until she takes his hand away from his face and they hold hands and drift off. They talk to each other in their dreams.

THE END